The Chinese Executioner

"I was once involved in a criminal affair whose hero cannot be regarded as a man of sound mind. Yet I was wrong to call him a madman. He wasn't mad, and experts eventually decided he was perfectly responsible for his behaviour. It was a strange case . . . strange and at the same time simple."

These were the words that impelled the author to return again to the restaurant in Yin-Yang to hear, and sometimes interrupt, the old Chinaman's story of Chong, the Executioner in a remote province before the rise of communism.

The account of the execution which leads to Chong's downfall, and of his past, as it emerges in the colourful ceremonial of the law-court at his trial, is indeed full of surprises. The crime of which Chong is accused is itself unusual enough, but what is really strange—so strange that the mandarins of the court never understand it—is the motive or obsession that lies behind it.

Pierre Boulle

The Chinese
Executioner

Translated from the French by
Xan Fielding

London
Secker & Warburg

Part One

Part One

I WAS sitting in a restaurant in the magical city of Yin-Yang. Before me stood a bowl of rice and three plates laden with exotic delicacies. A Chinese book lay open by my left hand. I would decipher a column of characters, then try to fish out a morsel of food with my chopsticks, both these operations presenting equivalent difficulties. After a lengthy tussle I shut the book and concentrated all my attention on the meal.

"There's not a single interesting suggestion in this novel," I said to myself peevishly. "It's the crime of a madman. I won't get anything out of it."

It was an utterly incoherent detective story. I realized with some embarrassment that I had spoken out loud. The old Chinaman sitting opposite was looking across at me with an amused expression. His chopsticks were poised in mid air and, branching out from his fist, seemed to trace a "V for Victory" sign above the table.

"Sir," he said in French, and in a sententious tone of voice, "there are some things that can't be learned from books."

"I know," I replied pensively. "There are many things that can't be learned from books: literature, for instance."

"Sir," he went on, "I gather you're intrigued by reprehensible acts. I heard you say something about a crime committed by a madman. Offences of that sort can sometimes be extremely interesting. I was involved in one myself."

I felt a thrill of excitement and examined the old gentleman with relish.

First of all I must tell you that I'm a professional writer and that in my profession I employ certain methods which are not universally approved.

My first rule is never to be spontaneous in my stories; never to yield to the demands of my mind (such weakness, to my way of thinking, being pardonable only in extreme youth) and thereby contribute to the hideous sin in which guilty old men recklessly encourage the writers of my generation. My second rule is never to observe what is going on round me. Thus my stories are neither the outcome of an inward urge, scorned out of modesty as a vulgar source of inspiration, nor an over-close examination of humanity, condemned as a crude indiscretion. I never write the truth.

My chief concern is to distinguish myself from others. With this aim in view, my particular plan consists in imagining *a priori* a peculiar situation which is utterly improbable by human standards. Above all, in fact, I do my best to achieve an *effect* of surprise; and when several possibilities of this sort come up for consideration, I naturally choose the one which presents the most outrageous and most inconceivable absurdity.

Then, taking into account that after all my readers are human beings, I strive to endow this situation with a deceptive appearance of rationality and to bring it to life by means of a false logical sequence which perfidiously tends to make it acceptable. I thus achieve a further factitious effect: the effect of surprise.

As you may suppose, the stumbling-block that constantly confronts me in this systematic composition is the main character. I have not succeeded in eliminating it entirely, and it almost always demands a model which one is apt to look for in real life. But how am I to take my characters from real life when I endow them with absurd reasoning? How am I to choose them from among us, since they have to behave in every circumstance like puppets?

I have got round this difficulty by drawing on the Chinese, an utterly unreal people, outside humanity though very much alive, who can supply the patient forger of facts with sufficiently extravagant subjects by the thousand.

This is simply to account for my presence after dark in the magical city of Yin-Yang. I feel so much more at home in a Chinese atmosphere. Sometimes, as on this occasion, I also venture into one of those improbable restaurants where the smell of rotten eggs mingles with the scent of spices, in the hope that a perusal of the surrealist characters that are to be found there will put me in a suitable frame of mind for the creation of those weird adventures which are my daily bread, and provide me with an artificial compensation for my total lack of sensibility.

But on this particular evening I was feeling uneasy and tortured by remorse. For several months, true to my word, I had not set foot in the city of Yin-Yang. Only the day before, after a paternal word of warning from my guardian angel, I had sworn never to enter its gates again.

My guardian angel always keeps a close watch over me. He is deeply hurt when I reject the models to which he is partial, and my escapades had alarmed him. He kept telling me over and over again:

"Beware, oh beware, of the twisting alleys and deadly lanes which make a treacherous spider's web of this city, a hazard for inexperienced souls. Put an end, I beseech you, to this pursuit of Chinese shadows.

"Paint men as they are, I implore you, and not as they have no business to be. Art has nothing to do with research. You frighten me when I see you toiling away among those dragons. Stop making such an effort. Let your heart overflow. There's nothing to be said for the weird and outlandish. Don't expect *chinoiseries* to be accepted as a literary form.

"The writer's art consists in reproducing familiar clichés, then embellishing them and embellishing them again, and finally setting them in a delicately chiselled framework. His talent is judged by the credibility of his characters, that's to say by the normality of their thoughts and actions. I anticipate your objection:

you're going to tell me that the Chinese do exist. That's a poor excuse. Don't imagine that a living creature is necessarily plausible. He must also have no unusual feature, no original quality, no peculiarity, and must also have been conceived like this by several generations of your predecessors and introduced by them in hundreds of works to which I can refer, before I can accept his plausibility. I know thousands of men and women like this on whom you could base a story, and your choice would be made still easier by the fact that in the long run they boil down to a mere three or four. I both chuckle and wince when I witness your vain endeavours to discover new characters and see you finally return from your quest with a synthetic monster, in whom it is all the more difficult to believe, in so far as his grimaces are vaguely, grotesquely reminiscent of certain human expressions. How can you hope to be convincing with Chinamen as your models?

" If you don't follow my advice people will begin to think you're nothing but a humbug, and that would mortify me."

I was naturally not in the least inclined to adopt these principles, but I have a high regard for my guardian angel's wisdom, experience and solicitude. One of us two was right. Since he has progressed beyond the age of doubt and reached that of mathematical certainty, he is convinced he's the one and not I. He had almost succeeded in convincing me as well. The grief I was causing him filled me with confusion, and that's why for several months, as I said, I had resisted the attraction that the city of Yin-Yang exercises over me—a praiseworthy feat, for this attraction is as strong as the lure of forbidden pleasures.

And this evening I had yielded to its spell. This evening I had not only filled my lungs with the noxious fumes that poison its atmosphere but I had entered a temple of extravagance where people eat with little sticks. This evening, as in the days of my most shameful excesses, I had supplemented these pernicious stimulants with an example of reading matter which has inspired me with the most trumpery plots: a Chinese detective novel.

I had given myself the excuse that I was taking no risks since I was on my guard. My escapade would not have any consequences. I would speak to no one. I would accept no suggestion without first subjecting it to the test of common sense. I had even cast my book aside with scorn as soon as I thought I detected a devilish whiff of fantasy in it which insulted my Cartesian nostrils.

And here, on his own initiative, was an old Chinaman engaging me in conversation! Here he was, talking about a crime: a crime committed by a madman, and presenting a certain amount of interest! I thought—I swear I did—of my guardian angel. I bit my tongue and maintained a heroic silence. But he persisted.

"As I was saying, sir, I was once involved in a criminal affair whose hero cannot be regarded as a man of sound mind. Yet I was wrong to call him a madman. He wasn't mad, and experts eventually decided he was perfectly responsible for his behaviour. It was a strange case."

"A strange case," I murmured involuntarily.

"Strange and at the same time simple, sir," he said.

I have said enough to indicate that the adjective "strange" exercises an unusual fascination over me. But when it is accompanied by the epithet "simple" my mind is seized by an absolute frenzy. In fact these two qualities, strangeness and simplicity, are more or less my only artistic criteria; the first, for the reasons of the effect to be produced which I've already explained; the second, for less base motives, which I have not yet been able to elucidate. On two or three occasions only have I encountered the coincidence of these virtues, which are difficult to reconcile but are not contradictory, and in each of these miraculous circumstances I have felt exalted to a superhuman pitch, infinitely closer to Olympus than to this sorrowful vale of tears. Once it was over a face . . . but I have sworn never to yield to an inward urge.

My good resolutions for the evening suddenly appeared somewhat exaggerated. After all, I said to myself in order to allay a faint misgiving, I can listen to him with one ear and still be free to forget whatever he has to say. One step more, and I had made up my mind not to let him escape until he had told me his story, even if I had to resort to force.

But first I decided to rely on diplomacy. I knew it was bad form, with men of his race, to betray too much curiosity. I pretended in a Machiavellian way not to show any more than a polite interest in his words.

"Really?" I murmured.

"Really and truly, sir," he replied.

After that I commended him on his advanced age. I know how to deal with the Chinese.

"Venerable sir," I said, "I'm a mere stripling, but I should like to benefit from your experience which, I feel sure, must be considerable."

"You're right, sir," he agreed. "My experience is considerable."

Then I asked him if he would do me the honour of sharing a flagon of *choum*, or rice wine, with me and declared myself ready to lend a humble ear to his reminiscences if he saw fit to acquaint me with them.

A furtive gleam came into his eye, then he heaved a deep sigh.

"It would be a pleasure, sir, for there are moments in a man's life when he feels the need to imbibe a little alcohol."

"I like that phrase," I said. "There are moments in a man's life . . ."

". . . when he feels the need to imbibe a little alcohol. That's a Confucian maxim."

"This evening I feel one of those fleeting moments has arrived."

"So do I; but I've already finished my meal, and ritual forbids the absorption of alcohol at this stage."

"Then let us start another meal, venerable sir," I suggested.

He thought the matter over and seemed to appreciate

the quality of this compromise. A waiter cleared the table and came back with a multitude of plates containing little bits and pieces of the diverse animal life that inhabits the forests, seas and skies of China. The bottle of *choum* was placed between us. Then the old man embarked on his story.

2

"SIR," he began, "this adventure occurred in the province of Li-Kang, where I was born and where I spent part of my life. The province of Li-Kang lies embedded between India, Tibet, Burma and the rest of China. The climate there is harsh, communications difficult, industry poorly developed, large towns scarce. For all this we're not savages. We abide by the traditions of the ancient and precious Chinese civilization. We have adopted certain Tibetan rites whose picturesque quality beguiled our forefathers, and in spite of our proverbial xenophobia we have accepted certain Western practices, brought back no doubt from India by our travellers, which seemed likely to enrich our ceremonies.

"Respect for one's elders is observed by us as much as the cult of one's ancestors. Wise men, men of letters, are held in high esteem. That at least was the characteristic of my province when I was living in Yi-Ping, and there is no reason to believe that the customs have since changed."

"Yi-Ping?"

"That's the main town, the seat of the provincial government, the town where I once humbly but honourably exercised the doctor's profession. But let me specify the degree of our civilization, for too many foreigners, among those who have not travelled, regard us as barbarians."

I told him that I had travelled and that my views were different. But he insisted on describing the various institutions of his province in detail. He laid particular emphasis on its legislation. He dwelt at great length on the perfection of the Chinese legal code and the wisdom of the mandarins responsible for administering justice. I listened to him with half an ear, impatient to hear him embark on his story. He was finally prevailed upon to do so when I declared that I could see no difference between the laws of Li-Kang and those of the most highly developed countries in the world.

"Well, I used to exercise my profession in the town of Yi-Ping and, as my digression may have led you to suspect, I was frequently called in to collaborate with the tribunals in the capacity of a medical expert. I appreciated this honour, but among the delicate tasks which made me a modest auxiliary of Justice there was one which afforded me no joy. In fact it was an ordeal, and it was only because I was impelled by a sense of duty that I could bring myself to accomplish it. This reluctance of mine was inexcusable; but perhaps you will make allowances for it when I tell you that I was required to attend all the capital executions in Yi-Ping and to direct them from the medical point of view."

"I absolve you, venerable sir," I said. "I can see only too clearly why you should have regarded that task as an ordeal."

"I am deeply thankful. . . . Well, sir, I shall now invite you to one of those grim performances, namely the one that took place at the beginning of the year nineteen hundred and twenty-one, according to your method of computation. I shall try to re-enact it for your benefit as faithfully as my memory permits."

These words sent a shiver down my spine as I thought of my guardian angel. I sighed. I knit my brows and, assuming my most solemn tone, declared fairly firmly:

"It's impossible for me to follow you on that course, venerable sir. You're trying to drag me off and lead me down the paths of temptation. I'm sorry about it, because you had whetted my appetite, but from now on all such fantasies are forbidden me. In no circumstances will I listen to the description of a capital execution, even though it did take place in China over thirty years ago, and actually in the province of Li-Kang, for whose civilization I have a high regard. I can see what you're up to. You're trying to achieve an effect of horror. It's a trick, and the most contemptible trick of all. Never speak to me again. Vanish out of my sight. I'll find some other source of inspiration."

But the old Chinaman did not vanish.

On the contrary, he made himself more massive and substantial than ever, and one of his chopsticks pointed at me like a peremptory index finger.

"I'm not striving after 'effects', sir. I'm telling you a story because you very politely asked me to do so, and because it gives me pleasure. If you find it unbearable, you are at liberty to block your ears, to think of something else and forget me, as a reader forgets a book

that bores him. As for vanishing out of your sight, I
find your request presumptuous, seeing that you're here
in China, in the town of Yin-Yang."

"Forgive me, venerable sir," I said. "I had no wish
to offend you. Your story doesn't bore me in the least.
But couldn't you eliminate such cruel and repellent
scenes as a capital execution?"

"I've got to make my story intelligible, and that
episode is indispensable. Besides, who mentioned
cruelty? I can see you have lent an ear to those legends
which represent the Chinese as inhuman creatures who
delight in certain refined forms of torture. You ought
to know that though the death penalty is applied in the
province of Li-Kang, the stake and other punishments
have been abolished ages ago. Our condemned men
are despatched with a minimum of suffering: by decapitation. We don't employ a perfected machine, as you
do, but the balance and temper of the sword, the
strength and skill of the executioner are such that the
operation is almost always performed in a single stroke.

"You ought to know, furthermore, that the death
sentence is only ordained by our tribunals for particularly serious offences and that, since the governor
indulges freely in his right to reprieve, necks are actually
severed very rarely in the province of Li-Kang—there
were no more than half a dozen executions in Yi-Ping
during the three years previous to the date at which
my story begins."

"Let's not talk about cruelty," I said. "I was wrong.
On the contrary, I defer to such moderation. I maintain,
however, that the ghastly details inevitably associated

with such scenes, however humanized they may be, cannot appear in any of my stories."

"Then, since that is your wish, sir, I shan't say a word."

"I spoke a little hastily, venerable sir," I hurriedly assured him. "You're quite sure your story is really strange?"

"Strange and simple, as I told you before. But you will never hear it, for your nerves are too delicate."

"Devil!" I exclaimed. "Tempter!—I mean, venerable sir! Will you at least guarantee that the logical sequence of your story demands this capital execution?"

"I guarantee it does, sir, and I am deeply hurt by your suspicions. I fully intended to pass over the more unpleasant details in silence and to concentrate on the essential facts which can't shock anyone."

"Is that true? Can I trust you implicitly? Are you certain these facts aren't upsetting?" I said, on the verge of capitulation.

"I give you my word that my story could not offend the susceptibilities of a child."

"I wasn't thinking of children, venerable sir," I muttered. "I was thinking of my guardian angel."

"Guardian angels, sir, are unknown in the Chinese world. I abide by the terms of my pledge: the susceptibilities of a child."

"Go ahead, then," I said submissively.

3

" ONE morning, sir, I arrived at the central prison of Yi-Ping well before dawn, with orders to attend one of those ceremonies whose description seems to horrify you somewhat unduly but which, as I said before, had no appeal for me at all.

" In the registry, which was the usual meeting-place, I joined the little group of officials who were subjected like myself to this ordeal. The room had been decorated the day before with garlands of brightly coloured paper, but was rather dimly illuminated by an oil lamp, the padellas and multicoloured lanterns having not yet been lit.

" There were various mandarins there, both big and small, each of them occupying a position in our judiciary administration which, with a few differences, has its counterpart in yours. I shall call them by the approximate titles which are familiar to you. There was the Mandarin President of the Tribunal, the Mandarin Attorney General, the Mandarin Police Chief, and the Mandarin Prison Director, not to mention the condemned man's advocate and myself.

" There were also the representatives of the various religions to which our people subscribe and which offer them a wide choice of godheads, devils, jinns and dragons. We Chinese are indifferent to religious fervour, but curious in matters of the spirit. Once our imagination is roused, captivated by the picturesque as much as by tradition, it is always ready to welcome a new fable provided its heroes are good enough to conform, as they generally do, to our centuries-old principles. Thus we resort to every possible cult when we feel that death is close at hand. That morning, I remember quite clearly, only three were represented—by a Buddhist monk, a Taoist priest and a sage versed in the rites of Confucius.

"Needless to say, there were also the executioner and his assistants.

"These officials, sir, derived no more pleasure than I did from the idea of the scene in which each of them had to play a part; in fact I am certain they all felt slightly sickened. There is no country in the world in which the taking of human life is made an occasion for merriment, and China is no exception. This duty weighed on us heavily.

"It was a duty all the same. We had therefore braced ourselves to carry it out with the utmost dignity. We all greeted one another very ceremoniously, in the fashion of our country, which is different from yours but perhaps is more appropriate for solemn occasions. It consists in bowing low from the waist, with both hands joined together and held against the breast. So as to give you a complete picture of the scene, I ought to mention that at the beginning of the year the early hours of dawn are bitterly cold in the province of Li-Kang and we were all dressed in heavy Chinese cloaks with wide sleeves. In spite of this I felt myself shivering."

The Chinese doctor broke off and brooded on this recollection. I was watching him closely and had no difficulty in visualizing the scene he conjured up: a group of Chinese, shivering with cold, muffled up in their long robes, their arms crossed, their hands tucked into their padded sleeves, bowing solemnly to one another in the chilly light of the prison. I shuddered myself, then drained my glass and begged him to go on with his story.

"After greeting one another, calling the roll and finding all present, we left the executioner and his assistants in the registry, and in single file, making as little noise as possible in our felt slippers, we made our way to the condemned cell which was situated at the far end of the prison.

"When we arrived, the brass band was already in position, standing silently outside the iron gate. Then, at a signal from the Mandarin President of the Tribunal . . ."

"The brass band?" I exclaimed, unable to believe my ears.

"Isn't that what you call a collection of drums and trumpets? There were also some brass bells, which come from Tibet, and other instruments whose names I don't know in your language but which you would recognize, I think—a sort of hollow wooden mill on the end of a stick which makes a loud clatter when whirled round in the hand."

"Rattles, probably. But what the devil . . . ! "

"If certain details are repugnant to you, sir, let me pass over them quickly.

"Well, the Mandarin President of the Tribunal gave the signal for reveille to be sounded. The fanfare burst out all at once, with the violence of an explosion, all the instruments going at full blast, making the walls of the ancient citadel vibrate. Then the cell door was opened and we went inside. The condemned man was already awake, sir.

"His bedclothes were in a tangle, as though he had spent a disturbed night. His hands were clapped to his ears, which was scarcely surprising, as the din was infernal. His gaze was fixed on the door. His eyes . . ."

"Please don't describe his eyes," I said, mopping my brow. "I'd sooner hear you talk about the rattles."

"As you like, sir. . . . Well, the rattles stopped, so did the other instruments, and the Mandarin Attorney General went up to the condemned man. He bowed low before him, told him what was in store for him, expressed his regrets and politely advised him to take courage.

"The condemned man showed a bold front. His limbs were trembling slightly but he managed to get up and courteously returned the mandarin's greeting. He dressed almost without assistance and was soon ready. We followed him outside. He was flanked by two guards and preceded by the brass band. Our procession filed down the dark corridors of the prison. That slow progress is somewhat grim for the witnesses, sir. It inevitably suggests a funeral procession, for the drums and trumpets play the same tunes in both cases. I never got used to it."

"I can understand your anguish, venerable sir. Put an end to it quickly."

"Eventually we found ourselves back in the registry. In accordance with the ritual, the padellas and paper lanterns attached to the garlands were lit by the assistant executioners. They formed a dazzling vault under which the condemned man was placed. This was the last stage before the scaffold itself, which was erected in front of the prison, in a courtyard separated from the room by a single heavy door. The musicians had stopped playing and had gone off by a roundabout way to take up their positions outside.

"At this stage the final formalities had to be fulfilled. These are reduced by the laws of our country to the minimum which decency requires. Mere respect for the human being demands the observance of a certain ceremonial; however abject the criminal may be, Society cannot get rid of him as though of a dangerous animal. So on that morning, as usual, the traditions were scrupulously followed. The joss-sticks were lit. The condemned man's signature was registered in several ledgers. He was politely asked what his last wishes might be. He was given permission to write to his family. The priests of the three religions offered him their services, one after another, then all together.

"He refused most of these favours and declared himself ready to die, his only request being to get it over as quickly as possible. I assure you, sir, he was a staunch character. His bearing was exemplary. He had even managed to suppress the tremor that had seized him on waking. I'm not saying this in order to move you to pity, but because it is an important element in my story. He was a vile wretch who had several human lives on his conscience; but we were grateful to him for his courageous attitude and for not bursting out into lamentations, entreaties and other tearful manifestations, which are always painful for those who are in duty bound to witness this torment to the bitter end."

"I can well imagine it," I said. "Those jeremiads must be most unwelcome."

"They are sometimes literally unbearable, but not in this case. . . . Well, the condemned man refused almost all the final palliatives, even declining the rice cakes he was offered.

"All he would accept was a glass of alcohol which, in accordance with the ritual, was handed to him by the director of the prison; but this, I must say, he accepted with avidity. He seemed hypnotized as soon as he caught sight of it. He snatched it out of the hands that held it out to him. He seized it so impetuously that a few drops spilled over, then he drained the contents in one gulp, like a drunkard . . . I think this eager haste should be forgiven him, sir. In a man's life, as I believe I mentioned before, there are moments when he feels the need to imbibe a little alcohol."

My old Chinese doctor paused for a moment and, as was evidently a habit with him each time he uttered this Confucian maxim, he gulped down five or six glasses of *choum* in a matter of seconds. Then his chopsticks clicked like the bones of a skeleton and he described a wide arc with his outstretched arm. In the twinkling of an eye he picked out several dainty morsels,

which he then dipped into some black sauce and
gobbled up in silence.

After taking a drink myself, I told him that I understood the condemned man's behaviour only too well
and found every excuse for it. Thus reassured, he
proceeded:

"Well, he drained his cup in one gulp and handed
it back with a brusque gesture. At this moment the
executioner, who had been hiding away in a corner,
emerged from the shadows and, after discarding his
outer cloak, appeared in the dress which is prescribed
by ritual: that's to say, stripped to the waist and wear-
ing nothing but long red breeches fitting tight round
the ankles. At the same time the Mandarin Prison
Director had the fire-crackers set off. . . ."

"Fire-crackers!"

"To indicate, sir, a new stage in the procedure of the
ceremony . . . the fire-crackers, and three strokes of a
monstrous gong which made us all jump although we
had been expecting it.

"I now find it indispensable to give you a further
detail and I beg you to pay the closest attention.

"At the moment the executioner stepped into the
full light—and in a most imposing manner, I assure
you, for this half-naked man, with his chest all red
from the cold and his legs in scarlet silk, introduced a
somewhat spectacular note among all our sombre robes
—at the same moment as the gong and the fire-crackers
pounded on our ear-drums and pulsated through our
heads, giving each of us the impression that the prison
was about to collapse, as the assistant executioners took

hold of the condemned man to proceed with the funeral
ablution and ritual make-up, the latter for the first
time betrayed his mental anguish. In spite of the din
I heard him give a low moan and I thought he looked
unsteady on his feet. If the assistants had not held him
up, sir, he would have keeled right over."

"I'm not in the least interested in these details," I
said. "You promised me . . ."

"They're an essential part of my story, and that
ought to make them acceptable.

"My colleagues and I exchanged a glance of anxiety.
We listened closely but there was no further complaint.
I thought—without displeasure, I beg you to believe me
—I thought that the condemned man had been seized
by a momentary weakness as a result of an overpower-
ing emotion, as frequently happens on these occasions.
This was not a novel occurrence in Yi-Ping. At previous
executions, I remembered quite clearly, the condemned
man had displayed similar faintness just at the very
moment, I beg you to note, that the executioner stepped
into the dazzling light created by the padellas and
lanterns."

"I can't understand why you should make such a
point of that, venerable sir "—he had laid a curious
emphasis on his last remark—" there's nothing *strange*
about it, as you claimed. This behaviour seems absolutely normal to me."

"So it does to me, and I'm very happy that our
opinion should coincide on this point. All the same I
must underline the self-control which the condemned
man had shown right up to that moment. The fellow's

bearing suggested a physical and moral equilibrium which was capable of withstanding every emotion right up to the final stroke of the sword. He was not the sort of man to fall into a swoon, like a woman with the vapours."

"And yet he fainted away," I observed impatiently. "I'm not at all surprised. I can't understand why you're being so mysterious about it."

"You'll understand later on, I hope. . . . But let me finish the most unpleasant part of the story.

"The assistants completed the ablution. They bound the condemned man hand and foot. They anointed his face with bright colours. The executioner bowed low before him. The henchmen dragged him off. The door swung back on its hinges. Another fanfare blared out. He was lifted on to the scaffold without giving any sign of consciousness.

"I shan't describe in detail the rites that followed. The final episode takes place while the condemned man's head is resting on the block. It consists of traditional kowtows, genuflexions, parades, Greek fire and burning incense, accompanied by music played to a faster and faster rhythm and with an ever-increasing volume until it reaches a sort of climax in which all the instruments, trumpets, drums, bells and rattles, break loose in the midst of a firework display of crackers and rockets.

"This lasts exactly a quarter of an hour. Then there is a minute of complete silence, and the executioner officiates."

"A quarter of an hour?"

"A quarter of an hour, sir, plus one minute. When the time was up, the executioner performed with his customary skill and competence.

"Then I approached. Hastily—rather too hastily—I examined the body and made out a certificate testifying death by decapitation. I was in a hurry to get it over, I admit."

"I don't blame you," I said.

"You are too kind. Others were less so. The ceremony having been brought to an end, and everything having taken place according to the prescribed ritual, we were preparing to withdraw, when something quite extraordinary occurred."

4

" AHA! " I exclaimed. " Something extraordinary? "
" Yes, sir. As the smell of the incense began
to fade in the early-morning light . . ."

"The incense? You're sure it wasn't a whiff of
brimstone? "

"I don't know what you mean, sir, but if my story
is too crude for you I may as well end it now."

"Traitor! You were saying something quite extraordinary occurred. . . ."

"A blast on a whistle from the Mandarin Chief of
Police, who was in the front row of the officials, as I
think I told you. This mandarin—a considerable figure,
the most important man in the whole province apart
from the governor—had appeared to take a keener and
more sustained interest in the execution than he usually
did: a suspiciously keen interest. Although he concealed his thoughts behind a mask of politeness, which
is a rule with us Chinese at any public gathering, it was
undoubtedly distrust that I had detected in his eyes:
distrust towards his other colleagues and particularly
towards myself. It made an unpleasant impression on
me. When the condemned man had moaned and then
lost consciousness, the mandarin had approached him
with an inquisitive air, shaking his head.

"Well, he gave a blast on his whistle while we were

still gathered round the scaffold, and in a moment we found ourselves surrounded by a troop of guards who had been hidden away in the corners of the courtyard. Then he asked us not to move and expressed his regret at having to detain us all for a moment or two: just long enough to proceed with his enquiry, interrogate us and take down our statements on the subject of the crime which had just been committed. He added that he apologized for laying this trap but that his sense of duty required him to catch the culprit, or culprits, red-handed."

"The culprits? Red-handed? I'm afraid I'm all at sea, venerable sir," I said.

"We were also all at sea," the Chinese doctor went on after a moment's silence, "and I don't think you could appreciate the extent of our perplexity or the irritating aspect of the dismay that seized us when the chief of police led us into the reception-room and posted his guards at the exits. Curious and apprehensive, we asked for some explanation. He hesitated, then, yielding to the pressing request of the two mandarin magistrates, he consented to reveal that it was a case of murder. He had been notified the day before by the governor of the province, who had received a denunciation and had ordered him, he once more explained, to catch the culprit, or culprits, in the very act."

"A case of murder?" I exclaimed with a start.

"A case of murder, sir. Those were his very words."

" And who was the victim? "

" For the time being he wouldn't give us the name of the victim or any other details. He withdrew and left us to ourselves.

" But put yourself in our place, I beseech you. Tell me if, on the face of it, and taking all the circumstances of time and place into account, you might not at least have toyed with the idea that the victim might well be the man whose head had just fallen."

" I'm more and more at sea. Didn't you tell me that the death penalty in the province of Li-Kang was . . ."

" . . . provided for and perfectly legal. I can see that at this very moment you're under the same misapprehension which was at the root of our anxiety."

" A misapprehension? "

" A misapprehension, sir. And if you ever write this story, which I can see you are already thinking of doing, I should like to draw your attention to the subtlety of the situation."

" No subtlety," I said firmly. " That's forbidden, and I'm likewise not allowed to demand the slightest intellectual effort on the part of my readers. Let's have a straightforward explanation."

" Well, we were undeniably on duty. We were sure we had followed the prescriptions of the law, but . . . Put yourself in our place, as I said before. Imagine that in the bitter cold of dawn, in the somewhat daunting atmosphere of a prison, after seeing a head fall as the outcome of a ceremony which I have only described

B

to you in part and which is something of an ordeal
after all, imagine that you had been requested to hold
yourself at the disposal of the courts to answer for a
murder, this particular case being a case of *flagrante
delicto*. You will then understand perhaps why we, the
most honourable men in China, were assailed by a
vague misgiving."

"I see you'll never be able to explain yourself more
clearly. Pray go on, though. I shall rely on intuition to
make up for a lack of logic which surprises me in a
man like you."

"One glance at us, sir, would have been sufficient
for you to discern the symptoms of that feeling of
oppression which I'm finding so hard to describe. The
two mandarin magistrates, who in any other circumstance would never have consented to losing face in
this way, did not raise the slightest objection. On the
contrary, they set a good example of submission to
higher authority. They advised us to be patient, pointing out that there was no possible charge against us.
They did so in such forceful, persuasive terms that I
felt they were trying to convince themselves.

"The Buddhist monk and Taoist priest were both
in a deep trance, in accordance with the prescriptions
of their respective doctrines. The Confucian sage, finding nothing in his science that could be applied to such
a violation of the rites, began to look rather disgruntled.
The Mandarin Prison Director had gone white in the
face, and I myself was not feeling too easy in my mind.
I confess I had to cross my arms firmly across my chest
to prevent myself from trembling. Such, sir, can be

the effect produced on innocent men under strain by a spectacular deployment of the machinery of justice."

"I'm beginning to see what you mean, after all, in spite of your obscurity, and I can well imagine the scene."

"But the executioner's attitude, sir, was the most remarkable of all. I was extremely surprised, because I thought he would have been hardened by his profession and able to control himself in the most trying circumstances. I must describe him to you, for this executioner plays a leading part in my story and he turned out to be a most unusual character.

"While his assistants, who were less affected than the rest of us, philosophically resigned themselves to being under close arrest, he, the executioner, betrayed signs of the utmost agitation. We could hear him talking to himself, muttering unintelligibly, then whimpering under his breath. All of a sudden he appeared to break down. He burst into tears and threw himself at the feet of the mandarin magistrates, beating his breast and crying out:

"'I'm the one, great mandarins, I'm the one who killed him! I'm the one, I tell you, and I also killed all the others in the last three years!'

"This statement was so ludicrous, sir, and the executioner's emotion so immoderate, that we were all deeply moved. It was an extremely painful sight for us and strained our nerves to the limit. The Mandarin Attorney General, a sensitive little man, began to display a similar lack of self-control and I'm certain I heard him mutter to himself: 'We did it! We did it!'

"The director of the prison likewise lost his composure and our group began to show every sign of the collective hysteria to which the Chinese are sometimes prone in spite of their robust mental constitution.

"A scandal was happily avoided by the Mandarin President of the Tribunal. He forced the executioner to rise to his feet, telling him sternly not to behave like a child and reminding him once again that he had only performed his duty, as we all had, which he seemed to have forgotten.

"We were somewhat reassured by the wisdom of these words, but the executioner still seemed to be out of his mind. He kept repeating over and over again, like a maddening refrain: 'I'm the one, I'm the one who killed him, as well as all the others!'

"At this stage the Mandarin President decided to put an end to this unseemly exhibition. He ordered two of his assistants to lay hold of him and keep him quiet. The executioner offered no resistance. After a while he calmed down and lapsed into a state of deep gloom.

"We were kept there, locked up and under guard, for about two hours. Then the Mandarin Chief of Police came back and got ready to interrogate us.

"He took possession of a small office and called us in one after another: first of all the Mandarin Attorney General, and then the Mandarin President of the Tribunal. Since neither of them reappeared, I concluded they had had no difficulty in exculpating themselves. I had no doubt that I should do likewise and I fortified

my conscience with the evidence of the facts. The three
ministers were ushered in, and after them the solicitor
and the director of the prison. I was left alone with
the executioner and his assistants, the latter quite
calm and unruffled, the former immersed in a grim
silence.

5

" IN my turn I entered the office and confronted the high mandarin. He expressed deep regret at being obliged to have me searched by two of his men. I complied with this formality with a good grace, so impatient was I to get the tedious business over as quickly as possible. The deep pockets of my outer cloak were turned inside out, its thick lining prodded. The sleeves were subjected to a careful scrutiny. Needless to say, the policemen found nothing of an incriminating nature. I breathed more freely. The mandarin looked disappointed. He dismissed his subalterns, made me sit down opposite him and, after the preliminary remarks dictated by politeness, delivered himself as follows:

"'Doctor, I'm going to speak to you quite frankly. A murder was committed this morning in the prison of Yi-Ping and the victim is none other than the man who was condemned to death. According to my information, this is not the first but the latest of a long series of attempts on human life which have been spread out over several months, perhaps several years. I confess, Doctor, that my suspicions first centred round you, given the nature of the weapon employed. So I must ask you a direct question. Was it you who administered the poison?'

"As you may well imagine, sir, these words, although

adding to my perplexity, served to dispel my apprehension. I was clearly the object of a definite suspicion and I should be able to exculpate myself with ease. I replied with righteous indignation that I had never administered any poison and had no idea what this was all about. The chief of police thought this over, made a note of my reply and decided to enlighten me further.

"'The denunciation sent to the governor,' he explained, 'maintains that capital executions are not being carried out in the proper manner in the city of Yi-Ping, and haven't been for some time. The condemned men are already dead, do you hear, dead and not only unconscious, at the moment the executioner fulfills his function. The source of this information claims that they are poisoned some time between reveille and the execution. That could only be by the hand of one of the officials. This morning, without your knowing it, I was watching you all closely. I could not detect a single guilty gesture, but I now know that the information is true. The condemned man succumbed to poison and not to the sword, which is against the rules of every civilized country and in particular those of the province of Li-Kang. I have scientific proof of the crime. The condemned man's body has been examined by a medical authority, and the expert is in no two minds about it: death by poisoning. . . . No doubt his was a rather more thorough examination than yours, Doctor,' he added, giving me a nasty look.

"This remark filled me with confusion—I whose professional honour was untarnished. I had to admit I had been guilty of negligence. My examination of the body had been extremely superficial. I was in a hurry to get it over and done with, and how could I have entertained the slightest doubt as to the cause of death? He that is without sin among us, sir, let him cast the first stone at me! "

" I would not be the one to cast it, venerable sir. Your haste is entirely excusable. Your oversight does not shock me. The question that defeats me is, which of those Chinese officials, which of those mandarins could ever have thought of taking such a step? And by what means? "

" By what means? The details are ghastly. I shudder at the very idea of them, but, while deploring the inevitable shock to a man of your sensibility, I can't conceal them from you.

" The poison, so I was informed by the Mandarin Chief of Police, a poison which was almost unknown in the province of Li-Kang, an extremely violent poison which annihilates its victim a few seconds after its absorption, had been mixed with the alcohol which is offered to the man condemned to death. . . . I'm surprised, sir, not to hear you voice your astonishment at this."

The Chinese doctor, who had uttered these words in a somewhat declamatory tone, was looking at me with an expectant, slightly disappointed expression, like an orator annoyed at having failed to produce the effect he has anticipated.

" The alcohol? ' I said dryly. " I thought as much."

" Sir, I was beginning to envisage that hypothesis myself, for the condemned man had not absorbed any other substance. What surprises me, though, is not that you managed to arrive at the truth entirely through your own resources, but to see you remain so composed and not even shudder with horror, as I did, when I heard the high mandarin methodically explain how some treacherous hand had made a lethal brew of that alcohol, that final favour granted by the humanity of our laws to the wretch who is about to die.

"I see you did not shudder at all. I wonder if your delicate feelings are not assumed and, considering all the fuss you made at first, I'm inclined to tax you with hypocrisy."

His gaze was fraught with protest. I felt I had to justify myself.

"Forgive me, venerable sir, but your story really is very strange; you said so yourself. I find it so disturbing that I can hardly tell when I ought to feel emotion or not. This isn't the first time I have gone astray in the process of reasoning, and confused logic with absurdity. You've succeeded in distorting my reactions in matters of sensibility. You see me completely at sea. I shall do my best not to commit any further blunder and to model my feelings on yours. But I wonder into what depths you're leading me."

"Sir, I don't quite understand what you mean. Never mind. From now on I shall stick to the facts."

"That's it, the facts," I earnestly agreed. "No one can be deceived by the facts. There must be some field of agreement between us, centred round the facts."

The old Chinaman shrugged his shoulders and went on:

B*

"An analysis of the few drops remaining at the bottom of the cup had confirmed the method used. The high mandarin had then suspected the director of the prison. The alcohol came from his cellar, and he was the one who had handed the cup to the condemned man. But, on being questioned, he had defended himself with such indignation that the police chief was prevailed upon to believe him. Besides, the flagon, which was still on the table, contained no trace of poison. The poison might have been introduced into the cup by any other hand, but not his. Furthermore, it was impossible to conceive of any motive which might have induced him to take such a step."

"A motive?" I broke in, raising my eyes.

"Yes, sir. The motive. Why are you looking at me like that? Surely you know that motive is a fundamental question in all criminal proceedings. In this case there appeared to be none.

"Nor could the chief of police think of any motive for the three ministers. On the contrary, the condemned man had declined their services, and their evident concern was to prolong his life as much as possible in the hope that the approach of his last minute on earth would bring him back to a sense of religion."

"I now admire your logic, venerable sir," I said.

"As for the two mandarin magistrates, he had only questioned them as a formality. It was obvious that neither of them could have the slightest reason to do away with a man condemned to death."

"What amazes me is how that high mandarin could ever have suspected you. I think I'm beginning to get a glimpse of your character, and I don't consider you capable of such a misdemeanour."

"I am grateful, sir, for your opinion. The same thought occurred to me and I respectfully pointed out to the police chief that I too had not the slightest motive of hostility against such defenceless wretches. To this he replied that men of science are always ready to try out a new experiment, out of love for their profession, and that just because this poison was so little known I might have thought of using it, as a dangerous test, on a man condemned to death. He went on:

"'In any case, Doctor, there's at least one charge against you in this affair. As a medical man, you have failed on two counts. You did not state that the condemned man was dead a quarter of an hour before the execution, which is contrary to the ritual. Secondly, you signed a certificate testifying death by decapitation, which is false. If you did not actually administer or even provide the poison, you are guilty of negligence, and it is in your own interests that I ask you to assist me in discovering the real culprit.'

"We Chinese are extremely punctilious in matters of ritual. A mere accusation of complicity could have got me into serious trouble. I was therefore prepared to do all I could to satisfy him. I carried my thoughts back to my arrival in the dark at the prison. First of all the officials had assembled in the registry. I had vaguely noticed the flagon of alcohol and the cup on the table. Someone had obviously introduced the poison in our absence: someone who had stayed behind in the room during the reveille ceremony. Then, taking into consideration the extraordinary behaviour . . ."

" The executioner! " I exclaimed.

" It stands out a mile. Yes, the executioner, or, at a pinch, one of his assistants. And when I recalled his attitude in the reception-room, there was no longer any doubt in my mind. In fact he had admitted it in so many words. A curious coincidence—that misapprehension which must be attributed to our incomprehensible emotion, had led us to misinterpret the significance of his behaviour.

" I was blinded by this revelation. ' The executioner! ' I exclaimed triumphantly, just as you did a moment ago. Needless to say, the Mandarin Police Chief with his professional lucidity had already come to this conclusion. He was merely trying to study my reactions, for he had not yet discarded the possibility of my complicity. My spontaneity appeared to satisfy him. All the other witnesses must have reacted in the same way. He asked me a few more questions, then dismissed me and called in the principal suspect.

" Our deductions were correct, sir. It was the executioner all right. His assistants were innocent. Having suspected the crime for some time, they in fact were the authors of the letter of denunciation.

" He repeated his confession, which this time left no room for ambiguity. He declared that he had always followed this procedure during the three years he had occupied his post. He had thus poisoned seven men who had been condemned to death. Seven murders, sir —a ghastly scandal! This had taken place right in front of my eyes, and I had never noticed a thing. I was therefore equally incriminated at the outset."

"You were equally incriminated?"

"Yes, sir. The executioner himself being unable to explain the motive which had prompted him to commit these acts, and even though he stated that he had acted entirely on his own, there was still some doubt about him in the mind of the high mandarin."

"The motive, I suppose?" I said, looking at him again in perplexity.

"Yes, sir, the motive. The executioner appeared to have no more motive than we did. I warned you, this is a strange story."

6

THE old Chinaman paused for a moment. I kept silent as I pondered on his story. Eventually he spoke again, looking at me closely.

"What do you think of my tale, sir? I see you are lost in thought."

"There are a number of points that bother me," I said. "You start off with the description of a macabre scene. You drag me into an obscure misapprehension of dubious morality. Then your story begins to sound like a detective novel. You dish up a murder and a murderer just when they are least expected. To crown it all, I notice you're not above indulging in dramatics."

"I was sure my story would fascinate you, sir."

"Not at all! You're quite mistaken. I'm criticizing it severely. I enjoy whatever is strange, but all this is gratuitously absurd in the extreme. You promised me simplicity!"

"And I maintain that I've kept my word," the doctor protested in an injured tone. "I maintain that my story is perfectly simple schematically. If you find it absurd, it's merely because you, sir, have lost your common sense. . . . An unexpected murder and murderer, did you say? You haven't even noticed that the victim was determined, marked down as though with a branding iron, from the very start. There's no deception. The

victim really is *the victim*, do I make myself clear?
And his executioner, you have to admit, is none other
than *the executioner*. There isn't any *basic* ambiguity
anywhere. My story is a crystallization of good sense
and straightforwardness."

"Traitor!" I muttered. "Seducer! O Satan, I recognize your insidious, bewitching logic-chopping only
too clearly. Yet I had sworn never to be caught up in
your snares again. . . . Yes, I admit, I am forced to
admit, that the substance of the story is simple. But
I should like it to be clearer still, if you see what I
mean. I should like its clarity to be evident to the least
sophisticated mind, without it necessitating the slightest
intellectual effort. I live in a world that doesn't appreciate *chinoiseries*."

"*Chinoiseries*, sir," said the old Chinaman, knitting
his brows.

"What I mean is, subtleties. Tell me quite frankly.
Is the rest of it sufficiently ordinary, sufficiently commonplace and conventional, for a child of twelve to be
able to appreciate its spice at a single reading? If not,
it would be better to stop here and now. I promised
my guardian angel not to welcome any further sugges-
tions for literary purposes."

"I can assure you on that point. There is no spice
in the rest of the story."

"So much the better, venerable sir," I exclaimed
with delight. "Yes, but unfortunately that's still not
enough. Unspiciness is necessary, but not sufficient.
While listening to you, I've too often had the sensation
of sinking into quicksands. Have you finished with

these sinister ceremonies, these traps, these cases of *flagrante delicto* and all this villainous police atmosphere? "

"You can set your mind at rest. From now on the Mandarin Chief of Police is going to vanish from the scene and be succeeded by the mandarin magistrates."

"That doesn't reassure me in the least, venerable sir," I cried out in dismay. "Mandarins of any sort could not possibly figure in any of my stories. Their feelings are always too lofty to make good reading. I should like to follow you, I'm dying to follow you, but you'll have to cast aside all the characters who represent authority in any way."

"That's asking a great deal, sir."

"I'm not the one who's asking it, venerable sir. If it was only myself I had to listen to! "

"I can't cast aside all the mandarins," the old Chinaman firmly replied. "In the province of Li-Kang a court of assize is inconceivable without magistrates."

"A court of assize? What court of assize? "

"Isn't that what you call the tribunals that try your criminals? Have I been so boring and unintelligible that you've already forgotten the executioner? His trial constitutes the whole framework of my story. But you are unnecessarily concerned about the mandarin magistrates. They only have a secondary rôle to play. They are merely there as the representatives of Justice."

"I see. All the same, venerable sir, my head is spinning, and even your promises send a shudder down my spine. You see me on the horns of a painful dilemma."

" Sir," said the old Chinaman, " will you kindly stop behaving like a child. Who's in charge here? Your rôle is to listen in silence . . . and say thank you afterwards. But since that's the way it is, I shan't say another word. My story ends here and now."

" Here and now! "

" The executioner stated he had acted on his own, without an accomplice. In the end they believed him, and I was only condemned for negligence and sentenced to pay a small fine. That's all."

" What do you mean, that's all. Why, you promised . . . ! "

" That's all, sir," he repeated stubbornly. " I was only condemned for negligence. . . ."

" But I don't care a rap about your sentence! " I exclaimed. " The executioner, what happened to the executioner? Can't you see he's the only one I'm interested in? Don't you realize that maniac is the saving grace of your story, just as other madmen occasionally redeem the sins of the world? You told me he acted without any motive? You give me to understand that he was tried as a criminal? And you mean to end your story there? "

" The trial was a great sensation, sir, and I could describe it to you in detail, for I was so fascinated by it that I noted it all down. But these *chinoiseries*, to use your own phrase, are unworthy of you. I'm very sorry. The executioner was an extremely peculiar character, quite out of the common run. His career affords some really extraordinary touches, which are all fresh in my mind, and calculated to entrance the amateur of the bizarre which I mistakenly thought I had found in you. Let's say no more about it."

"Demon! Stop playing with me, like a cat with a mouse. I must, I simply must know what happened to that executioner. I must hear the whole story."

Our relationship became somewhat strained. I cursed him up hill and down dale. I threatened him. But I soon saw I had nothing to gain by this outburst. In fact I am certain he was delighted to witness such a display of Western temper. I forced myself to be patient. I humbly apologized. I grovelled at his feet and begged him to go on with the story of the executioner. In the end he relented slightly.

"I will certainly go on with the story, since you appear so eager to hear it, but I lay down two conditions."

"I accept them without knowing what they are, venerable sir. Please go on. As for my guardian angel, to hell with him!"

"You seem to be in a more sensible frame of mind at last. These are my conditions. Firstly, since these facts were disclosed by the executioner himself in the course of his trial, I must drag you into those proceedings and, of course, introduce the mandarin magistrates who administered justice to the satisfaction of all concerned."

"It's sheer blackmail, but I said I'd accept it all. You've got the better of me. Drag me into anything you like, even into Hell. But go on with your story."

"Secondly, since I suspect you of hypocrisy and I don't wish to be accused of having inflicted a scandalous

subject on you by trickery—do you think I am as keen
as all that to tell you this story?—we shall now take
leave of each other. You will think the matter over and
weigh up your scruples for the space of eight days. I
shall be here at the same time next week and shall bring
my notes with me. Remember. In eight days' time."

I cursed my guardian angel, my doubts and my uncertainties, but I could not press the point. An old Chinaman is a difficult muse. This one was a particularly
tough nut to crack and required the full deployment
of my perfidy. I changed tactics and started discussing
commonplaces. He softened and we left each other on
apparently friendly terms, although he had not uttered
another word of his story. He would rather have been
chopped into little bits, like the food we had been eating, than make the slightest allusion to it again that
evening.

I went off with rage in my heart, feigning indifference.

And as I was leaving the magical city of Yin-Yang
in the dark, I came across my guardian angel who was
waiting for me in the moonlight, sitting on a stone and
preening the long feathers of his white wings to allay
his impatience and curb his anxiety.

He had not dared to venture into the accursed town
but, since nothing could be concealed from him, he
knew all about my conversation with the old Chinaman. He vented his indignation in reproaches which
were somewhat mitigated by his tone of paternal
authority.

"You wished me in hell, you cursed me," he said tearfully. "That I can forgive on account of your extreme youth. But here you are once again on the verge of committing a serious sin. Take heed of my warning, if not out of love for me, then at least out of respect for Literature, over which we stand guard—we, the angels, whom you had promised henceforth to serve faithfully, and to whom the meanderings of that old Chink with the Mephistophelean countenance are an outrage.

"I am prepared, charitably, to turn a blind eye on this latest prank of yours on condition that it does not occur again and that it leaves no written traces. Don't go to the meeting you arranged. Forget that impossible Chinaman. One more escapade like this, and you're lost. *Abyssus abyssum invocat.* I have trusted you up to now in spite of your whims, but another lapse will oblige me to abandon you on your downward path and even to rend you asunder."

"Listen," I implored him, "have pity on me. My mind is in a whirl. I feel torn between you and my old Chinaman."

"An executioner murdering a condemned man! Can you imagine it? In the first place, it's utterly improbable. I've never read that anywhere before. Secondly, it's irrational, since there's no motive behind it. Finally, even that yellow devil himself was cynical enough to warn you that the man in question was a rather unusual character!

"You must do as I say. I've told you a hundred times before: don't try to distinguish yourself from others—others greater than you have exhausted themselves at that sterile game. Abandon all pretence at research. You're at the age when a writer must guard himself carefully against those unwholesome impulses and concentrate all his energies on attaining the admirable perfection of normal qualities. The true artist can be recognized by his severity, by which I mean the patient genius he deploys to tame the demon of novelty in him and limit the originality of his work to the imperceptible vibrations which, on my charts, record the harmonious progress of the good old state of things."

There was so much benevolence concealed behind these stern words that I could not prevent myself from bursting into tears.

" I shan't do it again! " I cried. " I shall punish that Chinaman for his impertinence. I'll leave him to his rattles, his fire-crackers and his chopsticks. I swear I shan't go to that meeting."

My guardian angel's face beamed. He too shed tears of joy and gave me absolution. Purified and with a light heart, I returned with him to the world of moderation.

For a whole week, I aver, I applied myself to fortifying my mind in its good intentions. For a whole week, I declare, I followed my guardian angel's advice to the letter and punctiliously read a number of works he had recommended, feverishly trying to find in them some orthodox characters. For a whole week, I swear, I restricted myself to the company of dull, harmless people, and rushed off at full speed whenever I spied a countenance that differed in the slightest way from that of an ordinary person.

Part Two

1

AND eight days later, almost dying of boredom, I returned to the magical city of Yin-Yang.

Eight days later I found myself in the restaurant at the time the Chinese doctor had ordained. What am I saying? My mind was tortured with remorse, but I was there well ahead of time.

He, however, turned up at his leisure. He was carrying a brown leather briefcase, which he put down on the table. He displayed no surprise or satisfaction at seeing me. He greeted me in the Chinese fashion. I rose to my feet and returned his greeting automatically.

We were now sitting opposite each other, dipping our chopsticks into a mass of outlandish food which I had ordered on his advice. After the lengthy preliminary small talk prescribed by convention he told me he had assembled several documents dealing with the executioner's trial. He would be pleased to translate them for me since, apparently, I had decided to hear the rest of the story.

This last remark and the somewhat exaggeratedly courteous tone he had used, even for a Chinese, awakened my sense of dignity.

" Just a moment, venerable sir," I said. " Today it's my turn to lay down certain conditions."

For it would be wrong to take me for a weakling

with no determination, ready to surrender without a struggle to all the influences of the present occasion. I had come back to Yin-Yang, I admit, but I had taken my precautions. If I had abandoned many of my original objections, if I had ventured rather far along the path of renunciation, there was one point at least at which I would go no further; beyond this point all the Chinamen in the world would not be able to force me.

"I've given proof of my good faith, venerable sir. I have yielded to the fantasy of your reminiscences, but you must make some concession in return. I'll be absolutely firm on this point. If you wish me to listen to your story—and in spite of what you said, I can see that you are just as eager to tell it as I am to listen to it—promise me that it does not offend morality."

"Sir," said the old Chinaman, "what do you mean by that?"

I gave the matter considerable thought before replying:

"What I mean is this: promise me that it is not one of those infernal intrigues in which you can't tell Good from Evil."

"I promise," the old man said.

"Give me your promise, as a Chinese gentleman, that at no time do the wicked appear to be good or caressed by an insidious ray of light which endows them with a scandalous halo; that the good never behave in a manner to turn one's stomach by inspiring a disgust for virtue."

" That's a reasonable request. I give you my word, as a Chinese gentleman, sir."

" As in real life—I mean, our sort of life? "

" As in your sort of real life."

" I must go one step further. Will you swear that in your story there's a substantial barrier between vice and virtue? "

" I swear there is."

" As solid, as impenetrable and insurmountable a barrier as in the reality of our world? "

" Just as insurmountable, sir."

" Even that is not enough. You would still be capable of finding a loop-hole. I'm going to restrict the circle of your obligations with such a brilliant stroke that you won't have the slightest excuse for overstepping it. Swear again, swear on the head of your ancestors, swear that as in the real world—as in the real world in which I myself am living, do you hear?—it is the wicked on whom the hand of Justice will fall, and not on the good."

" That goes without saying, sir. I swear it on the head of my ancestors."

" One last oath, and I'm yours body and soul. Before all the gods in China, swear yet again that farce will not be interwoven with drama, that the grotesque and the tragic will retain their own respective character and will have no more in common with each other than Good with Evil."

" Sir, I swear it."

" You really mean it, you're not setting a trap? Exactly as in human relations? "

" As in human relations. Is that all? "

" That's all," I said, heaving a sigh of relief. " I can now listen to you with a clear conscience."

" The executioner's trial, sir, began about three months after the scene I've already described, and lasted several days. Let me first give you an idea of the setting.

" By some chance, about which there was nothing peculiar—it was rather an inevitable concatenation of circumstances—the officials playing the leading parts were the very ones who had assembled three months earlier in the prison of Yi-Ping to attend the capital execution. The Mandarin President of the Tribunal occupied the central seat, surrounded by several assistants. The Mandarin Attorney General was seated in the chair reserved for him. The executioner's advocate was also the same as before. As for me, together with the other witnesses of lesser importance, I sat in front of the public, just behind the bench of the Notables who made up the jury. Our regular presence there was not indispensable, but we had been invited out of politeness.

" We all wore national dress. That of the officials was in keeping with their dignity. The Mandarin President's robe was richly embroidered and adorned with several rows of rare furs. That of the Mandarin Attorney General, which was bright red, was adorned in the same way and from the front presented a large escutcheon of a dragon woven in gold and silver. These two dignitaries were likewise laden with necklaces and medals which weighed down their limbs and lent their gestures a ponderous majesty.

"Each of the mandarins was thus attired according to his importance. Each wore a skull-cap pierced with a red, blue or white pin to indicate his rank. Each wore a false beard and false pigtail of a length proportionate to his age. The Chinese have long ago done away with these accessories in everyday life, but they preserve them as symbols of wisdom and vestiges from ancient times. They bring them out on the occasion of a ceremony as important as a Court of Justice. Certain nations of the Western world do likewise, I believe. Each mandarin also wore brightly coloured make-up on his face.

"In the semi-circle formed by the tribunal, the Notables and the distinguished guests, only one man, sir, stood out like a sore thumb in this colourful gathering. He was distinguished only by the simplicity of his attire. He was dressed in the coarse drugget suit which the ritual requires him to wear. There was no bright paint on his face. Only his forehead had been smeared with white, the colour of mourning. It was the accused. It was the executioner. His name was Chong."

"What did he look like?" I asked.

"To begin with, he looked rather scared. I shall talk about him at greater length later on.

"The courtroom was richly decorated. But I believe you people attach less importance than we do to these artistic effects. I must tell you, though, that the walls were hung with heavy tapestries representing gigantic

dragons. The spaces in between were filled with long
banners on which were inscribed, in black characters,
some maxims of our greatest Sages, carefully chosen
to suit the occasion.

"One of these, for instance, which stretched from
the ceiling to the floor, proclaimed: 'It is an abomin-
able crime to disturb the established order.' Another
one read: 'Thou shalt not kill,' and yet another:
'Whosoever takes another man's life is as cruel as the
tiger of the forests, and a thousand times more contemptible, for the tiger does not know what he is doing.'

"Now this is the general procedure with us in this
sort of case. The hearing is public. The crowd usually
arrives well ahead of time and settles down on the floor
opposite the semi-circle. Then the accused, his advocate, the distinguished guests, the Notables and, last of
all, the Tribunal, take their place. This entry of mandarins is rather spectacular. A signal is given on the
drums and trumpets. The crowd falls silent. Everyone
stands up and remains bowed, with his hands held
against his breast. The accused prostrates himself.

"Then the mandarin magistrates appear in all their
pomp, one after another, with arms folded and head
lowered in a gesture of meditation. They move slowly
and in step. They come to a halt behind the chairs
reserved for them. They stand motionless for a moment,
turn to the right, then to the left, and ceremoniously
greet one another. After that they nod towards the
Notables, who bow before them. Finally they take their
seats and the crowd settles down on the floor again.

"The Mandarin President declares the session open.

He is the first one to speak. He puts his case succinctly and draws attention to the antecedents of the accused. In China, sir, the magistrates do not simply judge a man on the reprehensible act he has committed, they also try to shed some light on his entire life, going as far back as possible into his past, interrogating the members of his family, his friends and his enemies so as to reconstitute his whole personality.

"This was what was done in the case of the executioner. The Mandarin President devoted the whole of the first part of the morning to an account of Chong's childhood and youth and to filling in the gaps in the original enquiry with various statements of evidence. You will thus have the accused's character sketched out in broad outline for you, just as it was sketched out for us at the beginning of the session."

2

"THIS executioner, sir, this fellow Chong, was, as I said before, an extremely odd character, and some of his whims could well lend weight to the argument put forward by his advocate, namely that he was not fully responsible for his actions.

"Chong was born in Yi-Ping and belonged to an honourable and respected family: a family of executioners. His father, who had died three years before, was an executioner, as his grandfather had been. In China the posts of all mandarins, even the smallest, are hereditary. At this point, I remember, the President made a short digression to evoke his ancestors, render homage to their unblemished name, remind him of the examples he had had before his eyes, and lament at seeing one of their descendants on the bench of infamy.

"He had had a happy childhood, like most little Chinese boys. The statements of evidence covering this period of his life brought nothing remarkable to light, and nothing definite that could be held against him. At the most it appeared that he had evinced a certain shyness or oversensitivity which drove him to shun the games of his companions and resort to the society of weaker creatures: women, girls, and even, on occasion, domestic animals, for whom he showed an unusual affection. Though this trait in itself gave no cause for anxiety in such a small child, it should nevertheless be noted that instead of disappearing it became all the more pronounced as Chong grew older. No doubt it was deeply embedded in his nature.

"One of his former companions mentioned an incident which illustrated the development of this bent rather well and which the Notables, with good reason, considered extremely significant.

"Here is the statement of evidence of this witness:

"'One day, Mandarin President, I had gone out into the country with a group of friends. Chong came and joined us, which was unusual, as he scorned our amusements.

"'During the morning we set some traps of silk netting and, when I came back to lift mine after lunch, I was lucky enough to find in it, alive, a magnificent one-year-old pheasant. I was extremely proud, which was only natural, and all the others envied my dexterity. Before taking it out of the netting, I pulled a long needle out of my pocket and prepared to blind it by sewing up its eyelids, which is the usual method of keeping a captive pheasant and taming it easily. All my friends shrieked with delight and crowded round me to witness this operation, anxious to admire the feverish palpitations of the golden-plumed bird.

"'All of a sudden Chong, who had stood apart in silence, broke into the circle. He, who was usually so calm and placid, flung himself at me, Mandarin President, without my having done anything to provoke him, at the very moment that I was taking careful aim to insert the needle. Such was the violence of his

C

onslaught that I let go of the bird. He snatched it up and began freeing it from the meshes with nervous gestures. For a moment or two I was too surprised to move, for there was a strange gleam in his eye and he appeared to be in the throes of a violent emotion. Eventually I told him the bird did not belong to him and went up to recover my booty.

" 'Then, realizing he would get the worst of it, for my comrades in their indignation were ready to support me, he took a few steps back, released the bird completely and flung it high into the air. With anger blazing in his eyes he told us that it did not belong to anyone since he could not keep it for himself. In our righteous fury we gave him a good beating with a stick. But that did not get me back my golden pheasant, and I was deeply grieved.

" 'That is all I have to say, Mandarin President. That act revolted my adolescent heart. Even today I can only ascribe it to sheer spite and jealousy.'

"So much for this particular witness. Several others made similar statements. But after all, sir, one knows what these youthful outbursts of temper are like. They were acts of no particular import, which could be blamed on a spoilt childhood. Chong's mother had a weakness for her son and allowed him too many of his whims."

"I understand, the tribunal did not hold it against him."

"Of course not, sir. What an idea! It was not to

torment him that they were delving like this into his past. It was, as I explained, to get as complete a picture as possible of his mentality and to discover all the elements that might have influenced the evolution of his character."

"Your protest reassures me, venerable sir. Please go on. I'm also dying to get a clearer picture of his character."

"Chong, sir, never gave any real cause for alarm, and his family only began to get anxious shortly after he came of age, when his father applied for and obtained for him a position as an assistant executioner. This father naturally wanted his son to succeed him. He wanted him to embark on his apprenticeship under his guidance, which is the rule with all artisan families. . . . Have you any children, sir? I mean, have you a son?"

"No children, venerable sir. I take a fairly optimistic view of the fate of humanity, but not to the point of sireing a family. No son."

The Chinese doctor thought this over for some time, then gave a sigh and went on in a sententious tone:

"Nor have I, sir, but I think we are both deprived of one of the greatest joys in this world: the joy of seeing another self grow up who will prolong our own existence; the joy of directing his education, of transmitting our knowledge to him, of sparing him the errors into which we fell; the joy of re-living with him our first faltering footsteps, of seeing him hesitate at first, then master himself; the joy of teaching him in a few years what we took half a lifetime to acquire; the joy of seeing him gradually rise to our own level and—this must be profoundly moving—realize that he has equalled us, and of sensing him vaguely trying to surpass us in ability in the matters which we have taught him; and the final joy of knowing that our task is accomplished and of becoming the mute and anguished witness of a perfection which disconcerts us."

"You amaze me, venerable sir," I said. "I'm sometimes tempted to believe that you have a soul."

"Yes, sir, I've always regretted not having a son. Thus, despite my lack of personal experience, I can imagine as clearly as anyone what the father's despair must have been when he saw that Chong not only showed no inclination for the profession of his ancestors but actually performed his new functions as though they were an ordeal, appearing to be almost ashamed of them—rather like those sons of rich merchants who are embarrassed to serve or even be seen in their parents' shop, forgetting that it is the source of their fortune and respectability.

"To begin with, of course, he did not dare openly oppose his father's wishes, but he applied himself to his task with every sign of ill-will. The Mandarin President quoted actual details, which left no room for doubt as to his clumsiness, not to say his systematic negligence. His father having reproached him for his behaviour, he so far forgot himself as to reply—respectfully, it's true—that he did not feel it was a suitable job for him.

"'In point of fact,' the president here observed, 'it is only too clear that at this period Chong regarded himself as a creature of superior substance and had already been tempted by the evil genius of personal initiative.'

"These initial remarks inevitably shed an unfavourable light on the accused. In China, as you know, respect for tradition, for what is old and has survived the test of time, is the basis of all virtue. On points of detail, certainly, we allow Western practices, especially when we derive an immediate benefit from them; but our spiritual heritage must remain intact. In spite of the barbarous doctrines that have inundated us in the course of the centuries, we scarcely know any other religion than that of 'conversation', any other paradise than the citadel of the past. Despite all our dragons and countless jinns, there is only one Devil we really dread: the demon of change and novelty."

"That's not possible, venerable sir!" I exclaimed. "I'm absolutely hypnotized. I would never have thought that such a frame of mind could still exist in this world. I can hardly imagine it."

"It does, though, sir. . . . Even as a young man, Chong already appeared to be subject to dangerous impulses, and it was not long before there was no more doubt on that score.

"One day, when dealing with a condemned man who struggled and put up a fierce defence, he gave such a feeble, clumsy, pitiful performance that his father, out of shame for him, had to intervene personally in certain details of the execution which are specifically the assistants' responsibility, thereby losing a certain amount of dignity. The day after this exhibition Chong declared outright that he would not, could not, go on with this sort of job.

"He persisted in this decision with surprising determination, considering his usual lack of resolution, and in spite of the remonstrances, threats and entreaties of his father who was sick with anguish at the thought of losing face irremediably as a result of this abdication. Nothing would make him change his mind. The unhappy man therefore cursed his son and turned him out of the house. Then he locked himself up in his room to brood on his grief and humiliation. The wretched man's lot had a profound effect on the tribunal, which rendered homage to his memory."

"I am also deeply moved, venerable sir. But what about Chong, what happened to him?"

"He fled in shame. He was forced to leave Yi-Ping, and even the province of Li-Kang, where he had no friends and where he could find no means of livelihood, his conduct having been severely censured. He disappeared. For the next ten years all trace of him was lost, and the enquiry carried out in the town of Yi-Ping elicited only a few slender clues to this period. All that was known was that he had been in the far South and had had a rather hard time of it. . . .

"There were several reasons for this, sir," the old Chinaman observed, resuming his sententious tone of voice. "He knew no trade which could assure him a reasonable existence in our impoverished provinces. He had been brought up as an executioner, in a family of executioners. One does not break with impunity with traditions, bonds as strong as chains, everything that contributes to the formation of a man's personality. He had condemned himself by his own hand to live as an outcast. And so he languished, without parents, without friends, without means, no doubt in abject poverty, and one day, ten years after his departure, he turned up again in Yi-Ping."

"Just a moment, venerable sir. This executioner interests me even more than you think. I'd like to know what became of him during those years."

"He will tell us himself later on, at the request of the Mandarin President. I'm giving you the facts in the order in which they cropped up at the hearing. For the moment it's this president who is speaking, seated in his chair, leaning slightly forward, while a scribe unrolls before him a scroll of paper on which are inscribed the results of the preliminary enquiry.

"Well, Chong came back to his native city. He was in a pitiful condition when he humbly presented himself to his family. His rebellion, sir, had certainly not benefited him. You expressed the wish, in the name of your morality, that the wicked should be punished. No doubt you are feeling a certain amount of satisfaction at this point: he was reduced to skin and bone, in tatters, and covered with sores and dust. He was dying of hunger.

"He was ready, he said, to submit to his father's wishes and to resume his apprenticeship by his side. He even implored his father to allow him to re-enter the family house—him and his consort together."

3

"HIS consort! Venerable sir, I could hug you for that! God be praised! A woman! Your story, you must admit, was rather lacking in grace and gaiety. At last here's a somewhat less sombre touch. You didn't tell me there was a woman in it."

"There is, but don't rejoice too soon. A woman? His wife! At least that is what he called the wretched degraded creature he had in tow on his long peregrination across China. . . . Really, sir, that executioner had a peculiar character and was disturbingly attracted to all that was low. A demon must have inhabited him since birth, and it is not surprising he came to a bad end."

"Tell me something about this woman all the same. She interests me in spite of the abjection you mentioned."

"You will see her appear at the hearing, for a very short time anyway, the magistrates having deemed it unnecessary to hear such a witness except for the sake of form. But the Mandarin President felt it was worth while, at this point, to give us a rapid picture of her, this description serving to illustrate Chong's abnormal inclinations more forcefully than a lengthy speech. He also made a point of emphasizing how generous, not to say over-generous, the father had been in allowing him under his roof again together with this unworthy consort.

"You may perhaps know how attached we are in China to the appearance of our women. A plump woman is an honour for the whole family, whereas a skinny one is regarded as a disgrace to a respectable clan, since she can be got on the cheap. Well, Chong's wife, sir, was positively *scraggy* when she turned up in the town of Yi-Ping! Reliable witnesses had described her as a walking skeleton with hardly an ounce of flesh on her bare bones . . . and what flesh, sir! "

"Really, what flesh? "

"We are delicate artists, as you may perhaps have gathered, and all our poets have sung the fleshly tints of Chinese women, comparing them to the rosy petals of a flower which a butterfly scarcely dares to brush with its wings. Listen to this:

"'You are lovelier than apricot blossom bathed in moonlight; you are all the flowers and all the scents; you are the splendour of the world.'"

"I'm delighted, but not at all surprised, to find you're a poet, venerable sir. But, unless I'm mistaken, Chong's wife was not very like a flower? "

"Her complexion was leaden, sir: not the natural white of the hawthorn, but the deathly pallor of a corpse. She, too, was dying of hunger; but in addition to this she was diseased, diseased in the chest, and her sickly air inspired nothing but repulsion and disgust in anyone who saw her. Furthermore—I've kept the worst back till the last—she was blind! *Blind*, do you hear? As you know, we give our women names which extol

C*

the sparkle of their eyes, to honour one of their most obvious charms. We christen them 'Moonbeam' or 'Heavenly Star' or 'Sunshine'. Well, the eyes of this woman, sir, were filmed over and emitted not the faintest gleam. They were sightless!

" A diseased, emaciated cripple, and, to crown it all, a stranger—that was the wife he had brought back with him! As to how he had managed, on his long trek all the way from the southern provinces, to drag her, push her and carry her along, he subsequently gave a brief summary; but that mystery was never solved completely. Anyway there she was, by his side, like an insulting challenge to the harmony of this world, when he presented himself to his father like a repentant son. . . . And he wouldn't hear of being separated from her. Her admission into the bosom of his family was the condition he made for his own return to the hearth. In spite of his parents' entreaties he categorically refused to renounce her—he claimed to have married her legally —although he had every right to do so, for her disease was obviously incurable. He was barely prevailed upon, subsequently, since it was clear she would never bear him a child, to yield to his father's pleas and take a concubine. Even then it was only with extreme reluctance that he consented to this, and he did not keep her very long. . . . I am not playing any tricks on you, sir. I warned you this was a strange story in spite of its simplicity: scarcely credible at times, precisely because of the peculiarity of this executioner, this fellow Chong."

" Venerable sir," I said, " I can understand your

indignation only too well. I feel just as indignant as you do. I would give anything for this woman to have been attractive! But you have told me enough about her for me to be able to judge her unworthiness. My curiosity is satisfied for the time being. Don't give me any more horrible details about this ill-favoured creature."

"You are right. She was an outrage to Nature, and that's enough.

"Well, the father relented and took them both in. One could perhaps construe this open-handed gesture as a sign of weakness. But you must not forget that to him the return of his repentant son was a glorious compensation and to a certain degree wiped out the stain inflicted on his honour ten years earlier. Chong, moreover, must have been aware of this and was probably practising a sort of blackmail. The father accepted the humiliation of such a daughter-in-law as a lesser evil. We've no right to stand in judgement over him.

"He went further still. He saw to it that she was well treated under his roof. Thanks to his authority, she escaped the practical jokes which she would have had to endure in any other family for suffering from the handicap of such a vile personal appearance. Neither her mother-in-law nor the other women in the house employed her as a slave. On the contrary, following the orders given by the head of the family, who wanted her at any price to put a little flesh on, they absolved her of the more arduous household duties and went out of their way to cook her enormous meals in the hope of putting an end to the perambulating shame of her skeleton-like limbs. This diet led to nothing. She remained as skinny as ever and was still skinny at the time of the trial—skinny and, of course, blind."

"Such, sir, more or less, was the opening address of the Mandarin President. He spoke with complete impartiality. He maintained the attitude of objectivity which his functions demanded, and confined himself to the facts. These were sufficiently significant in themselves and needed no further comment. The accused's past appeared in a somewhat disturbing light. The Mandarin Attorney General had given several nods of disapproval. Counsel for the defence looked apprehensive.

"The president asked the accused if he had any objection to raise on the grounds of inaccuracy or any remark to make on what had been said about him and his wife. Chong could not very well deny what was known to the whole town and made a gesture to indicate that he had nothing to say.

"Then, sir, the second stage of the trial began. Since you have expressed your curiosity about them, you will now hear Chong himself describe some of his adventures."

4

THE old Chinaman opened his briefcase and took out several scrolls of paper.

"I have here," he said, "a more or less complete summary of the evidence. What prompted me to take these notes was the sensation caused by Chong's initial replies and the amazement at discovering the ingenuous and insane lengths to which that creature went to provide weapons against himself.

"Even today, sir, the reasons for this blindness are by no means clear to me. I know he had sworn to tell the truth—this practice, which you apply to witnesses, is extended by us to the accused—but no magistrate has ever expected a criminal to abide by his oath in such a rigorous manner when the truth is harmful to his cause. It's true that the most hardened cases are sometimes seized by a sort of madness which impels them to debase themselves, to make themselves out even more infamous than they appear to themselves in the terror and remorse of solitude. The judiciary annals mention cases of this madness, but no one had yet seen such a spectacular example of it.

"The defence, of course, could find in this very excess a fairly plausible argument for irresponsibility. . . . Perhaps, after all, the truth is to be found in that direction? Perhaps Chong already felt he was lost and imagined that only the extravagance of his conduct could save him from the sword? Perhaps this insistence on blackening himself was nothing but the supreme cunning of a quick-witted criminal trying to pass himself off as a madman? I'm not quite convinced all the same, sir, even though I saw and heard him. I don't think he was clever enough to put on such a show. I am rather inclined to think that he was not even aware of the effect produced by his words."

My old Chinaman fell silent for a moment, contemplating these visions of the past with an air of perplexity. Then he shook his head and went on:

" I'll leave it to you to judge. Listen to the conversation which took place between him and the Mandarin President after the usual interrogation to establish his identity."

He unrolled one of the scrolls and read me out his notes, commenting on them as he went:

" The Mandarin President began by asking the question which needed answering most urgently of all:

" 'Tell us, Chong, why you came back to Yi-Ping. Why, after showing such a spirit of rebellion ten years earlier, did you implore your father to let you resume your functions as an assistant executioner with him? '

" To this Chong replied:

" 'I wanted to become an executioner myself.'

" This, sir, caused quite a stir and gave rise to a certain amount of doubt as to his frankness, considering his former tendencies. The Mandarin President having expressed his surprise, Chong added:

" 'I wanted to become an executioner in order to perform the task more quickly.'

"At this point his advocate intervened. He could see the danger only too clearly. He hurriedly explained that his client meant to say: ' I wanted to equal, I even had the ambition of surpassing, by dint of application and dexterity, all the previous executioners, my predecessors, my ancestors.'

"But the Mandarin Attorney General in his turn intervened in the debate. He did not believe, he said, that Chong's words could be construed in this manner. He begged the president to make him explain himself more clearly. Chong looked round the courtroom. He listened, without appearing to understand, to the words which his advocate whispered in his ear. He pulled himself together and finally declared:

" 'I wanted to put the condemned man to death before the door of the registry was opened.'

"At that moment the drums went into action for the first time since the beginning of the hearing."

"So the brass band was still there? "

"Yes, sir. Drums and bells. The musicians were concealed behind a curtain, waiting to emphasize any sensational piece of evidence. And this particular statement was soul-stirring, I assure you. It was a confession of *premeditation.*

"As soon as the din died down, the President asked:

" 'How could such a scheme have ever entered your head, Chong? How and when? '

"This brought the executioner up short. He pondered on the question for some time and finally began speak-

ing, cudgelling his brains for the right word as though
he found it difficult to express himself. His statement
was rather muddled and the President had to unravel
it more than once. This is what he said:

"'It happened a year before my return to Yi-Ping,
Mandarin President, more than a thousand *lis* from
here, down in the South, in a small town in Yunnan.
. . . Yes, that's it, that's where the idea occurred to
me.

"'I was in extreme need. . . . My wife and I were
dying of hunger.'

" You will note, sir, that he had already saddled himself with that wretched creature. She was not inculpated,
but it was made clear very shortly that she had been
partly responsible for all his acts. . . .

"'We had already been through a long, extremely
long, period of suffering,' he went on. 'We were at the
end of our tether, without hope and in utter destitution.
I saw my wife slowly wilting away before my eyes. I
could not stand the sight any longer. I decided to put
her out of her misery, to make her swallow some poison
and then take some myself.'

"'What poison?' the Mandarin President enquired,
with a slight start.

"'I had a bottle with a black label, which someone
had once given me.'

"'Was it by any chance,' the Mandarin President
asked in a rather unsteady voice, 'was it by any chance
the same poison you used later on?'

"'Yes, it was the same, Mandarin President.'

"'In your own interests, Chong,' said the President,

silencing the murmur of the crowd with a gesture, 'you had better tell the whole truth. How did you come to be in possession of this poison?'

"'That's easy, Mandarin President. I remember quite clearly. I had worked for a time in the country, at a healer's. I was employed as his servant and he was very fond of me. He died in the course of an epidemic which ravaged the southern provinces. Shortly before his decease he sent for me, thanked me for having served him so loyally and presented me with this bottle. He warned me that it contained a deadly poison which he himself had concocted. He added, I remember, that he could not think of a more precious gift to make to a man like me.'

"'What did he mean by that?' asked the Mandarin President, voicing the general curiosity.

"'I don't know what he meant, Mandarin President. He had always been a good master, but he liked to tease me now and then, and he used to laugh at me when I brought home injured birds and shared my food with them. He died an hour later. I thought his mind was already wandering when he uttered those words and I paid no attention to them.

"'But I religiously kept the bottle to remind me of him. I thought of it when I had no more strength to endure my misery a moment longer.'

"'In the absence of any further evidence the tribunal accepts your explanation as to how the bottle came to be in your possession. Proceed, Chong, and don't omit a single detail. So you wanted to do away with yourself?'

"'That was my idea, Mandarin President. I had been thinking about it for several weeks. That evening I took the decision, for myself, for my wife, and also for a wretched animal, a sick dog I had picked up the year before, just as its master was about to have it put down. The man had given it to me in exchange for a handful of rice. I had enough to eat at that time; but for the last few weeks we had been living from hand to mouth, and the fate of that wretched animal added to our suffering and torment.

"'I was therefore determined to end it all that evening. I took the bottle out of the hiding-place in which I kept it.'

"'Was this with your wife's consent?'

"'Yes, Mandarin President. She had resigned herself to dying with me and the dog. We had nothing left in the world, and the owner of the hovel in which all three of us were living was going to turn us out next day to keep his pigs in it.

"'My idea was to start off with the dog. I didn't quite know the strength of the poison; I wanted to try it out on him. I poured a few drops out at random into a cup. I added a little water and offered the poor beast the mixture. I looked away. His plaintive look touched my heart. I can't bear the sight of suffering, Mandarin President. He had become extremely weak. He barely had enough strength to lift his head. My wife was in much the same condition.

"'With an effort he lapped up the drink. A few seconds afterwards I heard a short whine. Then silence.

I had to summon up all the courage I possessed to look round.

"'The dog was lying on his side. It had happened very quickly. A moment before, he was whining; now he was dead. He hadn't suffered, I'm sure of that. It was plain to see. A nervous twinge, an internal spasm which had accounted for the whine, just as an exclamation betrays our surprise when we bite into a sour apple; a second's giddiness, and that's all. His eyes had lost the pained expression which cut me to the heart. His gaping muzzle, now that his jaws were unclenched, no longer had the rictus caused by straining for breath. I felt a great relief to see him lying there like that, Mandarin President.'"

The Chinese doctor interrupted his tale to add a few explanatory comments.

"I don't know, sir, whether, in spite of my efforts, I've succeeded in giving you a faithful description of Chong's attitude and the impression it made on the crowd. He had implicitly admitted his foul intention in the most natural tone of voice, as though unaware of the import of his words, destroying by his own hand the only extenuating circumstance that a generous mind could at a pinch allow him: enthusiasm for his profession. He was suggesting, on the contrary, that he had chosen this executioner's job simply for the purpose of killing.

"He now described this ghastly scene as though he was re-living it in a dream, without manifesting the slightest repugnance. Whereas we were all deeply affected, not of course by the death of the dog, but because we vaguely discerned, though they were still wrapped in mist, the premises of criminal thought peeping through, he on the other hand did not realize how this factor was telling against him. I scrutinized him closely at that moment. I can still see him now. There he stood, unaware of the horror of his words, motionless, indifferent, detached and uncomprehending, isolated in the middle of a seething, murmuring crowd . . . a really incomprehensible creature, sir."

"Incomprehensible, venerable sir. Don't try, please don't try, to understand him. Don't let yourself be sidetracked by the difficulties of interpretation. Go on with your story. What did he say? What did he do? "

"He now seemed to be in a state of hypnosis. His pupils were distended and his gaze was fixed on a point in the ceiling above the mandarin magistrates, as though he was contemplating a vision. Nevertheless he answered all further questions.

"'Are we to understand, Chong, that the death of this animal exercised an influence on the acts for which you are appearing before us today?'

"'I'm not quite sure. . . . I think it may have done, Mandarin President, but I must tell you everything in the right order. I was all prepared to kill myself. The terror I felt at the thought disappeared at the state of peace suggested by this corpse. It seemed simple and easy. I seized a basin. I half filled it with hot water— we had not had any tea for a long time. I was going to pour the poison in: twice as much as for the dog.

We had agreed, my wife and I, to share the brew between us. I tilted the bottle. . . .

" 'At that moment, Mandarin President, I had a vision: a sort of dream, though I was wide awake. I had covered the dog's body with my old coat, yet I could still see his placid eyes with their sight snuffed out. . . . It was still the same dog, and yet it wasn't. I saw in front of me . . . it's difficult to explain, Mandarin President. I saw in front of me a man condemned to death—the last one, the one over whom I had proved so clumsy before my departure from Yi-Ping. I was spellbound by his eyes. I felt as though I was being sucked down with a ghastly whirl into the dark abyss of his distended pupils, while my colleagues slit his robe and tied his hands together. Not a single detail of his face escaped me. His complexion was the colour of the mists that rise from certain swamps. The door of the registry was thrown open and I could feel every tremor in his body, for it was my arm that supported him on the way to the scaffold. My own heart was pounding in time to his. I experienced, Mandarin President, I experienced the full horror of that final quarter of an hour, from the opening of the registry door right up to the end—the final quarter of an hour, and the one minute's silence.' "

5

"WHILE I'm about it, sir," said the old Chinaman, "it might be as well if I described the
ceremonial of this final quarter of an hour in greater
detail."

"Absolutely unnecessary," I said, shaking my head
emphatically. "I've got enough imagination to picture
it. Don't lose the thread. You're on the right track.
Go on reading me out the words of that strange
executioner."

"He expatiated, with a certain amount of obscurity,
on his hallucination—for that's what it was, there was
no doubt in our minds about it.

"'I can't express it clearly, Mandarin President. I
was looking into the very soul, the bared soul of the
condemned man; and there was also the dog with its
eyes at peace and its limbs at rest. There was nothing
else, I assure you, nothing else. . . .

"'And this vision arrested my arm. It crucified me.
. . . And all of a sudden I found myself contemplating
it with other eyes. All of a sudden, for no apparent
reason, I felt a shiver up my spine which was no longer
the manifestation of my horror. . . . I can't explain,
Mandarin President. All I know is, this vision put me
into another frame of mind and dispelled any intention
I had of suicide. I was now sure, yes, I was sure, that

life had not come to an end as I had thought a few moments before. I was standing upright, as though supported by some invisible hand, all my muscles flexed by some mysterious power. To live now seemed like a duty, a duty as imperative as veneration of one's ancestors—to live, Mandarin President, to live and return as quickly as possible to Yi-Ping.

" 'I put the bottle down and carefully recorked it.'

" We had all listened to this statement in complete silence, sir, and of course we were prepared for the question that followed:

" 'Was it at that moment that you made up your mind to resume your career as an executioner? '

" 'Yes, Mandarin President. . . . Yes, I think so,' Chong replied.

" Then, sir," the old Chinaman went on, running his finger along the cabalistic signs inscribed on his scroll of paper, so as not to miss a single one, " then the Mandarin Attorney General intervened. He rose to his feet and asked the President for permission to put a question to the accused. His request was granted. Chong twisted round slightly to face this new interrogator. The Attorney General spoke in a solemn voice.

" 'The accused has told us enough for us to hazard a guess as to his true intentions. It is now time he expressed himself without ambiguity. I ask him to describe what idea he had in mind when he recorked that bottle—carefully, as he informed us. Had he already determined his future line of action? Had he made up his mind to murder those condemned to death

by giving them poison, as we are entitled to assume?
Did he return to his home and resume his duties solely
with that aim in view, as his successive statements
suggest?'

"'Objection!' his advocate exclaimed. 'I object
formally . . .'

"'But why?' Chong chipped in, with greater alacrity
than one would have suspected in him. 'I can answer
perfectly well. On the contrary, I thank the Mandarin
Attorney General for having enlightened me by asking
me this question. I don't think I had ever thought about
it seriously. Without assistance I am incapable of solv-
ing the simplest problem. It has suddenly just become
as clear as daylight. I can see it now: the whole plan
had naturally taken shape in my head at that very
moment—the whole plan, except for a few details,
which I worked out on my return journey. It was this
plan which had taken the place of the dead dog and
the condemned man with the glazed eyes. It was this
idea which upheld me and drove me forward on my
homeward path and which gave me the strength to
overcome all the terrible obstacles I encountered.'

"'That will be all,' said the Mandarin Attorney
General, sitting down again. 'There's a clear-cut answer
for you. The court ought to be satisfied.'

"You can imagine how satisfied the court was, sir!
I can see it all again as though it was only yesterday.
The atmosphere was charged with horror. The revela-
tion of such perversity, the frank admission of such
cold-blooded calculation had caused a deep sensation.
Not only was there nothing in Chong's voice that

expressed the slightest remorse, but his eyes were gleaming like a fanatic's. This foul scheme, which a morbid hallucination had suggested to his mind, he appeared to regard with pride—as a mystic revelation inspired by heaven to enable him to work out his salvation. Yes, sir. An inveterate sinner, suddenly discovering a line of conduct which would put an end to his successive reincarnations and enable him to melt into the universal spirit, would not have spoken in more ecstatic tones than he did when he described the impulse which had driven him back along the roads of China to go and assassinate poor wretches in prison!

"The whole courtroom was appalled. . . . Some of your compatriots maintain that the Chinese are incapable of emotion. If you had seen us at that moment, sir, you would have realized the folly of such a statement."

"I *can* see you," I exclaimed, "I can see you all absolutely clearly!"

"It's when memories of this sort come back to mind, sir, that I go so far, I admit, as to imbibe a little alcohol."

His emotion was quite genuine. He asked me almost humbly for permission to interrupt his story for a few minutes. I granted him this respite all the more willingly in that his tale was beginning to disturb me as well, in spite of my cast-iron mental constitution.

After mastering his feelings, he continued:

"All the officials, although hardened by their association with the criminal mind, were astounded and scandalized by such cynicism. His advocate, having lost face, had nothing more to say and hung his head. The President, a very wise, experienced old mandarin, abandoned, probably for the first time in his life, the composure that becomes a judge. He was unable to control himself. He burst out, sir, as though he was one of the parties concerned and not an objective arbiter. For a moment even his robes were all awry. Picture him in your mind: an angry flush shows through his make-up and his false pigtail lashes the air from left to right. Listen to his words:

"'But after all, Chong, if an evil instinct drove you to murder, why did you have to gratify it on men condemned to death? I accept, I don't excuse, but I can at a pinch conceive, homicidal mania. I have known creatures who were destined for crime from their birth. But if killing was an irresistible urge to you, why in the name of heaven did you not attack the first person you came across? Why, when you already possessed the poison, did you have to embark on that long and arduous journey? Why did you pick on wretches already crushed by Destiny as your victims? Why this particular choice, which I find even more repellent than the act itself?'

"'Mandarin President,' Chong's advocate broke in, 'I would like this to be recorded as proof of my client's irresponsibility. He is suffering, it's clear, from a deformation of the mind, a fixed idea, which is characteristic of insanity. He is no ordinary murderer. He only attacks a limited class of individuals. He has never used his poison on anyone else.'

"'Perversity is certainly not an indication of insanity,' the Attorney General retorted.

"'Answer the question, Chong,' the Mandarin President persisted. 'We want a complete explanation. Why did you aim *solely* at men condemned to death?'

"'Why . . . ?' Chong repeated hesitantly, rather baffled by this outburst and trying hard to think. 'Why . . . ? That's another question I never asked myself. I'm not very clear in my mind on that point.'

"'Might it not be, Chong, the extreme facility which an executioner is afforded to strike down that sort of victim?' the Mandarin Attorney General suggested.

"'There's certainly something in what you say,' Chong replied. 'It did, in fact, seem so easy, so natural. I often wondered, I remember, why the thought had never occurred to me before, why no one else had ever had the idea. . . . That's absolutely correct, Mandarin Attorney General. I must thank you for clearing the matter up in my mind,' he went on, as though deeply relieved at having at last solved this problem. 'Just think! The cup of alcohol that is handed to the condemned man to give him courage, and just before the final quarter of an hour too! A mere gesture was all that was required. It was childishly simple. Yes, that's exactly what tempted me.'

"At these words, sir, the assembly manifested its disapproval by an angry murmur and even by loud exclamations which drowned the voice of the accused. It was late in the day and everyone's nerves were frayed.

The Mandarin President proposed an adjournment. The interrogation had not lasted very long, but the importance of the statements made up for its brevity. The Mandarin Attorney General agreed, but not before pointing out that Chong's cold-blooded reasoning was not by any means indicative of insanity. This was so evident after his reply to the last question that his advocate found nothing to say in his defence.

"The hearing was therefore adjourned for that day. The Mandarin President subsequently confessed that he had needed the whole night to recover his serenity.

"Let us follow the example of that Sage, sir, and have a short break, for I can see you are deeply moved. . . . Perhaps I was wrong to dwell at such lengths on the infamy of this scoundrel. Like all your compatriots, you will probably now make a sweeping generalization and judge all Chinese by the peculiar mentality of a single individual. Don't do anything of the sort, I beg you. On the contrary, you ought to regard the general reprobation provoked by his conduct as a striking proof of the instinctive horror that vice inspires in us."

6

THE maintenance of our cordial relations demanded a few words of encouragement on my part. I said to him:

"Venerable sir, you deserve a vote of thanks, for, contrary to what I feared, you're not trying to portray vice in glowing colours. The indignation inspired in your people by the ignominy of this fellow Chong sets my mind completely at rest as to the Chinese sense of morality. Please go on if you are not too tired."

He appeared flattered and proceeded with his tale without any further pressing.

"On the following day, sir, as soon as the hearing opened, Chong, at the President's request, went on with his story from the point at which he had stopped.

"'I put the bottle away, Mandarin President, with fingers that still trembled but with my heart infused with fresh courage. The images up till then had blinded my eyes to the squalor of the hovel. When they were dispelled, I noticed my wife's anxious face turned towards mine and I discerned an unvoiced question in her features. She is blind but she can sense a mood, and mine must have intrigued her. I recovered complete control of myself. I described my vision. It seemed to make a deep impression on her. She agreed with me that I should start off for Yi-Ping as soon as possible and resume my career . . .'

" ' You revealed your intention to her,' the President interrupted in dismay, 'and she did nothing to restrain you? '

" ' I simply told her my dream, as I told it to the court yesterday, Mandarin President, but even without being told she could feel the impulse that was driving me. The whole plan was agreed upon between us, without her requiring any explanation. On the contrary, she encouraged me in my decision. She too appeared to derive fresh strength from it. She got up, came over towards me and we remained close together for a long time, without speaking, holding hands, weeping and giving thanks to heaven for having metamorphosed our hearts. It was a great joy to feel supported in this way.'

" This declaration caused great astonishment. On further reflexion, the general consensus of opinion was that Chong, having realized he had made an unfavourable impression on the judges the day before, was now trying to redeem himself by laying part of the responsibility on this cripple. That opinion, I think, was mistaken. He must have been telling the truth. If he himself was capable of acting without external influence, this creature (a mere glance at her was enough) could very well have fallen in with any unnatural suggestion. Perhaps she was the only woman in the whole of China who was base enough for that. . . . And chance had brought these two creatures together, sir, chance or else one of those incomprehensible whims of a mysterious transcendancy which culminate in the order of the Universe and which Westerners do not accept, I believe."

"Yes, they do," I said. "Only they lump them all together under the name of Providence."

"Be that as it may, the President cut short any possible sly manoeuvre on the part of the accused. He told him in no uncertain terms that it was not the court's intention to inculpate a woman, a woman who was ill and blind. Chong heeded this warning with every appearance of the deepest respect and went on:

"'Having decided to stay alive, Mandarin President, we first of all had to find a means of implementing that intention. We had nothing in the world apart from the rags we stood up in and a couple of handfuls of stale rice. We could hardly crawl and we wanted to set out for the North the very next day. We had to have something to eat. We looked round to see what we could find. We ate the dog . . .'

"What's troubling you now, I wonder?" the old Chinaman asked, peering at me from under his eyelids which were screwed up in astonishment. "Oh, I see. The poisoned meat? They both thought of that, which proves they had recovered full possession of their faculties. They threw away all the animal's guts and roasted the rest of the body for the whole night, hoping that the cooking would render the poison harmless. It was a risk that had to be taken; they had to eat. On that point they won: they suffered no ill effects from it."

"I hadn't even thought about the poison. But to eat that dog!"

"I think your sensitivity on that score is somewhat misplaced. In China, where this story takes place, dog flesh is considered a most acceptable food. Eating a dog entails no sense of shame for us, and Chong could not incur any reproach from his judges for that particular act. So we were extremely surprised to see his eyes over-flow with tears as he recalled that memory. He, who until then had been intolerably calm and collected, now seemed to be suffering an untimely pang of remorse. . . . This fellow Chong, sir, was to disconcert us like this right up to the end of his trial, without prejudice to the horror he inspired in us. Not one of his reactions was that of a normal Chinese. Don't think I'm taking pleasure in inventing paradoxes, his attitude really was like this. He muttered a few words about this animal he had picked up, then burst into tears."

"I wouldn't dream of accusing you of gilding the truth, venerable sir. I am with you all the way, and without any reservations. Among all the oddities, which are my daily bread and which, as I can see, pullulate under the skies of China, you have found the ones which are most likely to satisfy my needs."

"I'm glad of that, sir, though I don't quite under-stand your enthusiasm. . . . But we now reach the point at which our two pilgrims set out for the province of Li-King—on foot, of course, because they had no money. An insane project. Chong described this episode in minute detail, which I shall merely summarize for you:

"Next morning, after eating as much as they could, and taking away the half charred remains of the dog wrapped up in a rag—their only possessions in this world—this cripple who could hardly stand and he, who

was himself unsteady on his feet, cut two sticks from a
hedge and set off along the dreadful roads of Yunnan,
making their way towards an inhospitable country
covered in lofty mountains. They embarked without a
second thought on a journey of more than a thousand
lis . . . I almost forgot!—in that old rag which served
them as a knapsack, there was also the bottle of poison.

"This bottle, sir, he hadn't forgotten it, you may be
sure! When he spoke of it a look of ecstasy came over
his face. You would have sworn that for him, for both
of them, it was a treasure more precious than gold; that
it contained within its depths a miraculous elixir capable of giving a sacred significance to the shameful
extravagance of their scheme, a philtre sufficiently
potent to make them forget their past suffering and
enable them to triumph over every ordeal to come.
They had taken infinite precautions so that it should
not get broken and so that not a single drop should leak
away: childish precautions which in any other circumstance might have provoked a smile and which Chong
described to us in solemn detail.

"They had manufactured an hermetic cork from a
knob of wood with a strip of cloth wound round it. This
had not been sufficient to allay their anxiety. They had
used the two wretched handfuls of rice they had left in
order to make a sticky paste which they smeared round
the neck of the bottle so as to make sure it was water-
tight. Then they—I say 'they', sir, because she helped
him. This monster of a woman was now taking part in
his insanity. Make no mistake about it, he was quite
honest in describing her eagerness as equal to his own

D

—they had worked part of the night on plaiting a coating of split bamboo, like those you sometimes find round precious bottles. And to safeguard this infernal potion still further, they had bundled the whole thing up in the still raw and bleeding skin of the dog: the skin from which they could have made a little money! Thus, to gratify their monstrous desire, they used up the sum total of their meagre resources. The evil powers that had taken possession of their minds inspired them with diabolical ingenuity.

"I saw you smile just now, when I spoke of an elixir or philtre. Having received a modern education, I understand and share your scepticism. But if the truth be told, every now and then ancient legends cross my mind in spite of myself. I find myself dreaming that the country healer who gave him the present might well have been a sorcerer and that he had added to the liquid a magic distillation as pernicious to the mind as to the body. You would excuse these meanderings if you had heard this fellow Chong accounting to us for his strange behaviour with painstaking care and describing, in tones that I cannot hope to reproduce, the throes he suffered at the thought that this bottle might be destroyed.

"In spite of my imperfect description, can't you visualize them all the same, just as I can imagine them myself? Can't you see them embarking on that dreadful journey, of whose perils they were well aware, with their shapeless parcel on their back, solely impelled, according to Chong's own statement, by the desire to kill?"

"I can see them, venerable sir," I exclaimed fervently. "I can see them both. I would be able to see them even if I were blind, and I would never be able to forget them. I don't need the use of my eyes for that. The forcefulness of your description is like an inward illumination. I can see them, I tell you. Your story is getting better and better."

7

HE acknowledged this homage with a bow and unrolled some more scrolls.

"Chong described his journey in detail, sir, first of all in reply to the President's questions, then carried away by his recollection of it. He seemed, in the end, to derive great relief from getting it off his chest. This lasted during several sessions, and the tribunal listened to the whole of his tale with its customary patience, and with the zest of interest to which his initial revelations had given birth.

"The journey lasted the best part of a year and was dreadfully arduous. I'm afraid I would tire you if I told you all the catastrophes that occurred. Most of them, in fact, offer very little food for your curiosity. They are adventures that inevitably happen to travellers of that sort, adventures whose essential repercussions on human nature can always be summed up in the same monotonous words: poverty, hunger, thirst, fatigue and fear."

"Poverty, hunger. . . . Do they all have the same flavour, then?"

"Almost all, sir."

"Venerable sir," I said, "your story has not been very cheerful, and here you are announcing further miseries. Yet I'm weak enough to be interested in these repercussions, which you appear to despise, of adventures on human nature: these interferences between chance events and organized consciousness. Aren't there any which are likely to throw your hero's character into sharper relief?"

"Some of these incidents, on the contrary, make him appear even more incredible."

"That's what I meant, venerable sir."

"Let me see now. . . . There's one, in particular, which you might like to hear, because there's an element of comedy about it for a change."

"A comic incident, venerable sir? Tell me about it quick."

"Here it is. It's the story about the brigands who . . ."

"Venerable sir!"

I had shuddered as I thought I had discerned, in the heavy atmosphere of the restaurant, the rustle of wings by which my guardian angel announces his presence. I must have been mistaken, for he never ventures into the city of Yin-Yang; but my dormant scruples were roused as a result.

"Venerable sir," I implored, "a story about brigands! And after the detective novel too! Just as I was beginning to believe you were on the right track! You're going back to the turgid stream of implausible vulgarity. Brigands are literally impossible."

But the old man asked me, in a rather sharp tone, not to start fussing all over again. Our relations, which had improved considerably, were in danger of becoming strained once more. I did not have enough strength to embark on a fresh quarrel. I took refuge in my cowardice and let myself be carried a little further along the forbidden path. In any case he had already resumed his story, without paying further attention to me.

"It was a month after their departure, sir, that this incident occurred. You must take my word for it—I'm the first to deplore the fact—but brigands still exist in China, and certain provinces in the South are infested by them, especially that part of Yunnan which our two pilgrims had to cross. Our honour and our dignity are not affected by this rabble, for they are not countrymen of ours but belong to a number of barbarian tribes which at one time came down from Tibet. That does not stop them holding up Chinese travellers all the same.

"Up till then Chong and his consort had been travelling through a fairly fertile and relatively civilized region: the plateau of Yunnan. There are plenty of farmsteads there. In one or another of them they had always been able to find a sheltered corner in which to spend the night, and even a little food after they gnawed the last bones of the dog. Although they were unsuited to rural labour and unable to provide anything else in exchange for this talent, they managed here and there to glean a handful of rice or the remains of a meal: enough to keep body and soul together. The Chinese are kind-hearted people, sir.

"Their luck changed when they came to the end of the plateau and reached the mountains that cover

Northern Yunnan. That's where the kingdom of the brigands starts. The few cultivated fields that are still to be found in the foothills are guarded night and day by the militia. A little further on it is all forest, intersected only by a few steep paths along which travellers never venture except in convoy and with an armed escort. For all these precautions, they are frequently attacked.

"Chong and his consort, however, did not hesitate to set off alone across this wilderness which barred their path. They could not join a convoy. The pace of the mules and foot-travellers was far too fast for them. The blind woman stumbled at every step, which is hardly surprising, for these paths, dotted with pot-holes and rocks, are hard going even for a man in possession of all his physical faculties. Chong was obliged to guide and support her constantly, so that they progressed at the speed of a tortoise. And they had a journey of a thousand *lis* in front of them!

"So there they were, stumbling up the first slopes. In point of fact the brigands were the least of their worries, which is not hard to understand. The latter do not usually attack wayfarers who are completely destitute.

"Yet they were held up all the same. They thought they had nothing on them which could rouse anyone's rapacity, apart from a few meagre provisions which they had begged from the farms before leaving the plateau. They were mistaken, sir. There was the bottle! That mysterious bottle, full of a colourless liquid like alcohol and wrapped up with a wealth of precautions which made it look like a precious flagon—the brigands were going to seize it in the hope of a carousal.

"This is where the comic incident I promised you occurs. Chong, who had surrendered all their food supplies without lifting a finger, although those few handfuls of rice and manioc represented several days of continued existence, suddenly snatched up the bottle, leaped away, took up a position with his back against a tree and defied his assailants. He blankly refused to pay this ransom, saying that he would rather be killed, and his consort with him. (It's a great pity, moreover, that the brigands didn't kill him!) He took a firm grip on his stick, he told us, ready to defend his bottle to the death, and the wretched cripple whom he called his wife placed herself at his side, imitating the threatening attitude (these are his own words) of her husband. This is how he described it.

"'We felt endowed with superhuman strength, Mandarin President, and capable of dealing with any foe. We were not in the least afraid. We brandished our sticks in such a fearsome way that the bandits were intimidated and abandoned the idea of robbing us.'

"In such a fearsome way! Can you picture the scene, sir? That band of lawless and godless ruffians, armed to the teeth—can you imagine them being *intimidated* by the grotesque demonstration of those two decrepit creatures reduced to a shadow by their privations? You can't believe it: a mere child would have had them at his mercy. To hear him give this mystifying description, you might have assumed, and

with good reason, that the brigands had been disarmed
not by their belligerent attitude but by the irresistible
laughter which seized them, as it seized the assembly
and even the tribunal at the mention of such an outrageous absurdity. . . . Doesn't it make you laugh,
sir? "

"Don't bother about me, venerable sir. I'm laughing
inwardly. That's a habit of ours in the West."

"It was to this laughter, almost certainly, that they
owed their salvation. For, it's a fact, the brigands agreed
to leave them their bottle and not molest them any
more. Their leader, however, laid down a condition.
Both of them were to undertake to act as their servants
for an unspecified length of time. Contracts of this sort
are often negotiated with these barbarians. Chong
agreed. He forthwith turned as docile and submissive
as ever.

"But have you thought of the trick he could have
played on them? It struck every one of us at this stage
of the interrogation. Do you know that at the sight of
the bottle all the men had brought out their drinking
mugs? If, instead of persisting in a stupid show of force
which could logically only end to his disadvantage, he
had pretended to comply with good grace to their
demands, he could then have given each one of them
a tot of this liquid which they had mistaken for alcohol.
He would thus have got rid of his assailants there and
then. Better still, he would have found himself in
possession of the two mules they had with them, not to
mention their load and any amount of provisions. He
would never have had to account for his action. The

D*

law is not so rigid in those mountains as in our civilized districts. The police are not up to much there and it was a case of legitimate self-defence.

"The whole of China would have applauded such an ingenious manoeuvre. Do you realize that even in their pitiful condition they had a fortune in their hands? A mere flick of the wrist, and they could have come back to our province as wealthy travellers and not as tattered beggars. Chong's family and all the Notables of Yi-Ping would have welcomed them with open arms. Furthermore they would have brought back with them a delightful story which would have met with universal admiration. . . . But no, sir. They thought more highly of this benighted potion than of fame and fortune, their own lives or saving face. They disdained this windfall. They let the opportunity slip through their fingers and preferred to come to an arrangement whereby both of them were turned into slaves."

"Incredible stupidity," I said.

"That's what we thought, sir. Incredible stupidity, or else criminal folly which annihilates every other sentiment, including the instinct of self-preservation.

"So they started working for their masters. The latter employed them on the foulest tasks and treated them worse than their mules. They dragged them along with them on long nocturnal expeditions and made them carry heavy burdens. On reaching a halting place, they had to prepare the camp, look after the animals and cook the food before being allowed to rest. That was what their life was like. They accepted everything: the most repulsive chores, insults and blows. They were

intractable only on one point, sir—the bottle. Listen to
these words of Chong's. They illustrate his diseased
mind rather well:

" 'At night time, Mandarin President, we had trained
ourselves to sleep by turns, and whichever of us was on
watch used to guard the bottle. Our precautions were
not superfluous, for it had incited the rapacity of some
of the men. They were intrigued by our stubborn
attitude about it and by the care we took to keep it
safe.

" 'I was worried to see a sort of legend taking shape
round it. They began to look upon it as something
endowed with mysterious powers. Often, in the evening, they would gather in a group not far from us and
converse in whispers, pointing at us with their fingers.
I tried to catch the drift of their conversation; it was
difficult, for among themselves they spoke a language
that was different from ours. But they all believed, I
know, that the bottle contained a magic elixir, the
possession of which would bring them great wealth.

" 'After the first month of our captivity, almost every
night shadowy forms kept prowling round us in the
hope of catching us both asleep. We would talk in a
loud voice and generally that was enough to scare
them off; but on one occasion, Mandarin President, I
had to fight with one of them who had sworn to rob us.
He was stronger than I. I was about to succumb; but
while he held me by the throat, bearing down on me
with his full weight, my wife bit him so violently that
he gave a yell of pain and woke up all the others. The
brigand chief came up to us. He was a man of honour.

He flew into a rage and upbraided his men. He ordered them to abide by the terms of the contract. Thus we miraculously kept our property.'

"In fact, sir, according to the disjointed explanations which Chong added to his statement, it seemed to us that the chief, too, had come to look upon this mysterious liquid as a talisman. You see the suggestion of magic cropping up again? It was impossible to escape. The frenzy which took possession of the prisoner, who was usually so calm, as soon as they tried to lay a finger on the bottle, would account for this sentiment in superstitious barbarians. The brigand chief may have feared neither god nor devil, but the colourless liquid no doubt suggested nothing good to his mind. As a responsible leader, he had to be on his guard against the vengeance of the jinns of the mountains if his men happened to get hold of it by means of a ruse contrary to the agreement. That's about the only rational explanation for his attitude, which Chong regarded as a miraculous intervention. Whatever the reasons, he made his authority felt and the treasure remained out of danger from then on.

"Chong and his wife spent several months with the brigands—three or four months, he could not tell exactly how long. He appeared to regard this captivity in retrospect as a period that was not too bad on the whole. When the attempts to rob them ceased, he told us, they had been less unhappy than in the town where they had lived before. The brigands always had enough to eat and their left-overs provided abundant meals. Some of his statements even tend to suggest that he was not far from regarding their capture as an occasion for rejoicing:

"'During this period, Mandarin President, we had hardly a care in the world and we ate regularly every day. We put on weight and recovered our strength. We adapted ourselves to the harsh conditions of the mountains and to physical fatigue. My wife even trained herself to clamber up the steep slopes unaided, feeling her way along with a stick. Without this apprenticeship we should have been unable to surmount the ordeals which were in store for us on the rest of our journey. We were well aware of this, and that's why we made no attempt to escape any earlier. Later on we felt that those brigands had been a godsend. But for them we should never have been strong enough to reach the province of Li-Kang, and I should have been prevented from accomplishing my mission. . . .'

"He occasionally spoke like this, sir, in a state of almost religious ecstasy. He used the word 'mission' to describe the dreadful task he had taken upon himself when he was raving one evening; and the hardships he endured throughout the journey, he frequently referred to as 'tests'. There was a strange gleam in his eye when he uttered these words, a gleam that was like —this is monstrous, but I have to admit it—like the gleam you see in the eyes of our saintly hermits when the hour of annihilation approaches as a reward for a virtuous life. I can picture them both at night time, under the stars, dreaming of this mission and impatiently waiting to recover enough strength to accomplish it!

"When they felt they were sufficiently fit, and having

acquired a fairly thorough knowledge of the mountains, they resumed their march towards the North. They succeeded in escaping. They seized the opportunity one evening when the brigands were all drunk, and sneaked out of the camp without being observed. They took nothing with them but a few provisions and, needless to say, the bottle.

"They marched all that night and all the following day, wishing to escape any possible pursuit. In point of fact, judging by his description of the brigands and by the fatalism that is generally found among adventurers of that sort, I feel sure they did not bother to run after them. Perhaps the chief was even happy to be rid of them and their talisman, which sowed discontent among his band. But they dared not risk a further postponement. Towards evening, after scaling a pass, they reached an inhabited valley. Only then did they halt, exhausted but delighted, as he told us in that incongruous language of his, at having triumphantly passed this initial 'test'."

8

"THEY started off again first thing in the morning. They spent no time in the valley, which was an oasis in this mountainous desert. They did not want to lose a moment. They made their way instinctively towards the North, as though the pole of their monstrous desire had inscribed invisible magnetic lines for them through the chaos of ravines and defiles.

"It was yet another folly: they were thus drawn towards the highest peaks of the range running down from Tibet, towards the passes which the caravans avoid, which only an occasional smuggler uses and which are snowbound for most of the winter. But the usual route for travellers meant a détour of several hundred *lis*, which their impatience would not accept. Chong claimed to have weighed all the difficulties and to have then decided to forge straight ahead, firm in the belief that heaven would not abandon them.

"The most extraordinary part of the story, sir, is that they succeeded. I don't know those mountains, but from the accounts of the few explorers who have been there they are enough to make one shiver with fright and they have a bad name in the whole of Southern China. Above a certain altitude the paths peter out and one can only move forward by following the river beds. Higher up still one is above the level of the forests and one finds oneself lost in a wilderness of jagged rocks, the very sight of which inspires terror. The climate is unhealthy. The sun hardly ever appears. Grey clouds and pernicious mists hover perpetually over the slopes, seeping into any living creature that ventures there and rotting the sparse vegetation."

"It's a description of Hell you're giving me, venerable sir."

"At all events a not very hospitable country, sir. Yet they clambered up those slopes bristling with obstacles! And they lived up there for several months, eating wild plants and repellent animals! How did that sickly blind woman manage to get across those ridges? And, on top of it all, she had a relapse. She started coughing and panting as soon as they reached the level of the mists. That climate and the strain were obviously anything but beneficial. He was soon obliged to support her, to drag her along, and sometimes even carry her when she was completely out of breath.

"She showed great courage, he told us. We can well believe him on that score, as well as when he describes his own hardships and suffering, proudly asserting that they had both gone beyond the limits of human endurance. He had sworn to tell the truth, and we must give him his due: no one detected a single falsehood in his statement. All the evidence goes to show that in crossing those mountains in such conditions they accomplished a feat which surpasses one's imagination."

My old Chinaman fell silent and contemplated his

chopsticks lying like two parallel bars on the table-cloth. He seemed to be harassed once again by one of those profound thoughts which contracted his muscles and expanded his cheeks. He leant over towards me. His physical tension manifested itself in a number of sententious remarks, to which I listened with as much curiosity as to his story.

"If those two creatures, sir, had been impelled by the spirit of *Good* instead of being possessed by a demon, they would have been capable of accomplishing the most sublime feats—I'd stake my life on that, as the saying goes. If only they had performed the same actions under the impulse of a noble ideal, all the inhabitants of China would have glorified them as heroes or as saints, so strongly do exploits of this sort appeal to the masses in my country.

"How they had managed to deploy such energy, such tenacity, such courage even, it must be admitted, with such an ignoble aim in view, constitutes a problem of a philosophical order which is liable to give rise to disturbing reflexions. While listening to the account of this arduous, tragic odyssey—an odyssey which, by virtue of certain signs of devotion, was occasionally admirable in itself—the whole court was plunged into a state of intense stupefaction which left no room for any other sentiment. After our greatest sages, I also tried to throw some light on this case by applying my knowledge of the human species to it, and also my experience of disease. I could not discover a single satisfactory solution. I find it hard to accept that the spirit of Evil alone could have dictated this heroic conduct. I find myself sometimes dreaming that there was some other incentive—a motive?—the motive which Chong had never been able to reveal and which perhaps lay buried in the innermost depths of his subconscious."

"Stop worrying about it, venerable sir," I told him. "You're cudgelling your brains to no purpose. If there's some obscure point in all this, neither you nor I will ever clear it up when the Supreme Court of Yi-Ping with its wise magistrates and notables was incapable of doing so. It would be presumptuous of us to try and tackle this enigma. Please go on."

"I shall only describe their crossing of the final pass, the highest of all, and above all what happened to them shortly afterwards, for it is rather remarkable.

"For several months they had been walking, stumbling, dragging themselves along, striving despite their suffering to climb slightly higher every day, drawing closer every minute to that pass which opened the road towards the Promised Land. For several weeks they had not seen a soul, and what food supplies they had, which had been patiently hoarded with this hazardous crossing in mind, were quickly running out. At night time they slept huddled close together in a fissure of the rocks.

"They managed at last to reach the pass before winter, before the great cold and the snow, and started descending the further slope. But they were in such poor condition that they soon had to stop. They had gone, as they put it, beyond the limits of their endurance, and the woman's disease had flared up again.

She was half dead, he told us. Here are his very words:

"'A pernicious mist had penetrated her lungs and was devouring them, Mandarin President. She could no longer move. She sank down at the foot of a rock. She mumbled a few words. By placing my ear against her mouth I understood that she was begging me to abandon her and go on without her to the province of Li-Kang to fulfill my mission there. I refused to do this. I felt we were both engaged on this mission and that I needed her to bring it to a successful conclusion. The cold suddenly swept over us, for this slope was not protected from the winds. Night was falling. The first flakes of snow thickened the mist. We could not go on, yet a lengthy halt meant death. I thought we were going to perish there and, just as I was beginning to give way to culpable despair, Mandarin President, I had a proof that heaven had not abandoned us.'

"Heaven again, sir, you notice. He had adopted this sacriligious mode of expression once and for all.

"'I lay down beside her so as to afford her some shelter. A gust of wind pierced a gap in the fog. I noticed thirty yards below us the outline of a roof. This apparition was so extraordinary in this wilderness that I thought I was raving, suffering from an hallucination caused by overstrain and the approach of death.'

"He took great pains to describe the fantastic nature of this apparition. Depending on the swirling mist, it was sometimes buried in deep snow and sometimes emerged like a ghost through a thin transparent cur-

tain. His idea of a mirage was understandable. The
blind woman could be of no help to him. He rubbed
his watering eyes until he was convinced that his mind
was not wandering.

"There was a hut there, no doubt long abandoned,
but still in fairly good condition, set into a mass of
rocks which protected it from the storms. Some
smugglers had probably built this refuge at some time
or other to serve them as a halting-place in the days
when the illicit traffic between the provinces was at its
highest pitch. The roof, made of rough branches, was
half rotten but still kept out the rain and snow except
for a few drips. The walls, which were of the same
material, afforded reasonable shelter. A fireplace had
been erected in the middle—a raised patch of trampled
earth, like those in our country cottages. In one corner
there was an ample store of dry wood. It was a provi-
dential asylum, and some excuse can be found for
Chong's state of mind when he still believed it was a
miracle even after recognizing the reality of his vision.

"He had great difficulty in struggling to his feet and
carrying his companion to this refuge. He laid her down
on the floor, where she collapsed unconscious. He tried
to light a fire and only succeeded after several attempts.
He was trembling from head to foot. He heated some
water. He managed to make the sick woman swallow a
few mouthfuls of the brew which for many unfortun-
ates takes the place of tea. He could do nothing more
for her. He sat motionless in front of the fire, contemplating this wretched creature who, from all appearances, had no more than a few hours to live."

"A sad vigil, venerable sir," I said.

"Extremely sad, sir. He gave us a heart-rending account of it. Night had fallen. Outside, a storm had broken. The room, lit only by the fire, was gradually invaded by thick smoke. There are no chimneys in these bothies. Drops of icy water kept dripping on to them at irregular intervals. The woman, her features drawn and her limbs contracted, gave no sign of life except when she was occasionally racked by violent fits of shivering. As for him, he remained crouching by the hearth, too exhausted to sleep. He too began to feel the first effects of fever. His teeth started chattering. He was suffering from all the fatigue accumulated during the past months. His eyes wandered from the prostrate form by his side to a corner of the hut where he had wedged the bottle between two logs. . . . What thoughts could have run through his head in this tragic situation, between this dying companion of his and this devil's potion, at a time when he was on the verge of collapse himself, knowing he was in a benighted region far from all habitation and that they had hardly any food left? He was not able to enlighten us on this point. He claimed that the fever had dimmed his memory.

"For he was the one who fell seriously ill in the end. And the woman did not die. On the contrary, she recovered very quickly, as you'll see presently. . . . Those disinherited, sickly and decrepit souls, sir, whose life seems to hang on a thread, always manage to find in the innermost depths of their unworthy carcases some resources which paradoxically prolong the period of their outrageous incarnation on this earth, whereas sturdy, healthy people are carried off by the slightest infection. I've often noticed that."

"Such venerable sir, is the absurdity of this world."

"As you say, sir, and we can do nothing about it. . . . Anyway, she recovered, and rapidly. The next day he felt weaker and weaker and did not move from his position except to rekindle the fire and put some water on to boil. She sat up all of a sudden. Some colour returned to her cheeks. She spoke in her normal voice. He realized she was alive and felt, he told us, an intense joy. But at that very moment he was felled by his illness and lapsed into unconsciousness."

"This journey is certainly no pleasure trip," I said.

"I warned you, sir. They spent some grisly days up there, it can't be denied. I can understand how you feel. While listening to Chong's account of his misfortunes, we too experienced a similar sensation. The cruelty of the Chinese is, as I told you before, a legend. We are capable of being moved by human suffering as much as any other race. In the present case, I give you my word, we really had to reason with ourselves, to remind ourselves of Chong's villainy and the aim he had in mind, not to let ourselves be carried away by a culpable compassion."

"I'm having to make that effort of memory myself. But will this tragic situation soon come to an end?"

"It will become still more tragic, sir. For in this refuge which they had looked upon as a gift from God, they presently endured a ghastly torment, more terrible than sickness and want. I could skip this incident if your susceptibilities . . ."

"Hypocrite! Tell me about this torment. I can't imagine anything worse happening to them. What is this fresh atrocity? "

"The rats, sir. A frightful scourge in certain provinces of China."

9

"RATS, sir," he went on, "are a plague in China, and in that hut they had no protection against them: they slept on the bare floor, without bedclothes, and the wood fire was their only source of light.

"The day after they arrived, while he was watching over his companion, a single rat had put in a furtive appearance. Half its stiffened body had emerged into the room through the branches when Chong, who was dozing, caught sight of it.

"'It didn't make a sound,' he told us, 'it didn't move an inch.'

"His glance had fallen at random on this inquiring snout. He had the sensation that the rat had been there for some time, for several hours, peering, listening, sniffing, spying with all its faculties on the new inhabitants of the hut. He was overwhelmed by a superstitious terror which paralysed him for a moment. He more or less told us that this vermin appeared to him like a demon bent on mischief and deliberately detailed by Hell to foil his scheme!

"Chong's mind, mark you, was populated by phantoms. He was instinctively inclined to attribute an occult significance to the most trivial natural manifestations. It's true that excessive suffering and privation might have affected his brain. I can easily imagine

him being fascinated by that rat, fancying he saw in
it the incarnation of some malevolent Power. And this
illusion persisted.

" In the end, however, he shifted his position. The
rat at once disappeared as discreetly as it had arrived.
It did not show itself again that day, neither it nor any
other like it, and the night went by without further
alarm. Only the following evening they appeared in
vast numbers. At that time Chong was prostrate on the
floor, in the throes of fever. It was the blind women, sir,
the blind woman who had miraculously come back to
life, who with her unsteady hands had succeeded him
in kindling the fire, it was she who withstood the
assaults and who, in the darkness in which she lived,
fiercely defended their few mouthfuls of food and the
flesh and blood of their bodies; for these animals are
ferocious.

" When he was not completely unconscious, delirium
made him confuse these beasts with the chimeras of
some other world. So the account he gave us of these
battles was somewhat disjointed. As you can imagine,
the sight must have made a deep impression on someone in the throes of fever. I've noted certain passages
which are nevertheless of interest:

" ' The demons made their infernal power felt shortly
after dusk, Mandarin President. I can only remember
some of those nights. I've lost all recollection of the
others.

" ' I was lying by the fire, shivering the whole time
in spite of the heat, my body as heavy as lead. It began
with some strange noises above our heads. They came

from the thick layer of decaying twigs which formed
the roof; they sounded like the whispering of malevolent
spirits preparing a foul scheme in the dark. My heart
turned to stone. I saw my wife's face stiffen. She was
gripping her stick, standing stock still, her body leaning
forward, trying desperately to sniff out from which
direction the threat would come. But our enemies
formed an unbroken line. The whole roof heaved and
creaked, as though infused with a life of its own. The
din grew progressively louder. Some sharp little cries,
betraying hideous delight, made me quake with fear,
as a ghostly chuckle might have done. I, I who had my
sight, could soon discern more and more numerous,
more and more aggressive undulations which swept
over the walls of the room and vanished into the
shadows. I knew they were creeping down and closing
in on us. My wife did not move. I made a desperate
effort to raise myself up on one elbow and explore the
floor all round us, in the terror of finding one of the
monsters there and in the certainty that they would
soon all be there. She sensed my fear. Feeling her way,
she threw some more logs on the fire.

"'The attack was not slow in coming. As always, it
took me aback. As always, it occurred in an unfore-
seen manner. Sometimes quite close, in the full light
of the flames, at other times brushing my limbs as I
struggled to peer into the furthest shadows, one of these
creatures would rise up, its pointed snout motionless,
its cruel red eyes fixed on us as on a selected prey. Once
again it had escaped my notice. Invisibly, as though
by magic, it had crossed the illuminated patch.

" ' I gave a groan. My arms felt so heavy that I could not lift a finger in defence. The rat jumped aside. It mocked me with a somersault and vanished into the shadows. My wife had heard and understood. She turned her head carefully in the direction of the caval-cade and started laying about her with her stick which clattered on the hard floor. At the very moment she put the first one to flight, I noticed another behind her which had come up as silently as its predecessor and was spying on us with the same patient and relentless air. I shouted to put her on her guard. She came back, sweeping the ground all round her. At this stage a rustling sound warned us that a whole army had imperceptibly advanced. Leaps and grotesque somer-saults announced a general movement of withdrawal, a retreat exactly sufficient to put them out of range of the blows delivered at random. . . . There was calcu-lation in these manoeuvres. They knew quite well that she could not see them and that I was paralysed! They withdrew a few paces at the most. They formed a circle barely larger than the illuminated area. I could make out constellations of red pin-points scrutinizing the clumsy hand that wielded the pathetic weapon. When a flame rose a little higher than the others it cast terrify-ing shadows on the ground.

" ' I saw some enormous ones, bigger than cats, more horrible than dragons, all animated by the insatiable thirst to do harm. They were *intelligent*, Mandarin President, intelligent, perverse and well organized. Their assaults were synchronized. They relieved one another, battalion by battalion, so as to allow us no

respite. They tried to overwhelm us by presenting themselves in the most grisly forms that their genius could
imagine. Their very appearance sometimes brought a
cry of terror to my lips, and the diabolical cunning of
their countless manifestations deceived my wife's attention. She got up. She made the rounds of the room,
feeling her way along, tapping on the roof, on the walls
and the floor. The brisk ebb and flow of the reserves
lying in wait in the filth prolonged the sound of the
blows. The whole hut was haunted by Spirits bent on
our destruction. She had not finished her rounds before
others had already crept into the middle of the room,
mocking her erratic sweeps. They laughed at her
infirmity like naughty children. Repulsive masses
brushed against my legs. My shudders scarcely drove
them off. The blind woman came back, not daring to
strike any longer for fear of hitting me. Her anxious
hands felt my body. She clung to me. She confined herself to brandishing her stick in all directions, while I
informed her whenever I could of the most pressing
danger. We could only think of protecting a minute area
round us.

"'Then they embarked relentlessly on a harassing
series of forward thrusts and withdrawals. Sometimes,
when my companion's arm grew tired, when she no
longer had sufficient resource to vary the intensity and
extent of her blows, when the monotony of her efforts
increased their audacity, the circle of seething flesh
closed in so far as to engulf us, like the hands of a
strangler with a thousand fingers. Sometimes the vice
loosened a bit, when she summoned up her strength

and when one of the demons, struck by chance, did a somersault and gave a sharp cry which sowed momentary alarm among the serried ranks. But order was quickly restored, under the effect of a stubborn persistence, of a superior authority. The monsters would then launch themselves at us again.

"'I can't remember how many nights my wife spent like this. I frequently lost consciousness, my head buried in my arms. Can you imagine her then, Mandarin President, alone, facing this accursed army in the dark?

"'She could tell from my silence and my posture that I had closed my eyes, and was of no more help to her. She redoubled her vigilance, went out of her way to make up for the handicap of her infirmity by the sharpness of her ear, by that sense of danger which blind people possess, and by *reflexion,* Mandarin President. . . .

"'It was, as I said before, as I know, a battle of wits. She concentrated all her faculties on varying, in a thousand different ways, the extent, speed and threatening impression of her blows. She racked her brains at every moment to invent an original detail in her series of gestures, an unusual tone in her shouts, and each discovery of this sort, by narrowing the field of innovations, made the next one all the harder. Our lives depended on the strength and speed of her imagination. At every moment her mind had to assemble the elements of an effect of surprise, for rats soon grow accustomed to anything. She had to surpass them in cunning, deceive them by giving them an impression of unflag-

ging watchfulness and keen sight. She confessed to me
later that her efforts resulted in a torture that was
harder to bear than the physical strain.

" 'If she relaxed her vigilance for a second, as sometimes happened, we would wake up covered with these
foul animals which chewed up our clothing and nibbled
our very flesh. One night, I remember, Mandarin
President, I had succumbed to one of my torpors. I
had a dreadful nightmare. I dreamt that a legion of
dragons had entered my chest and were eating out my
heart. I suffered this horror for a very long time,
paralysed by disgust and pain. When I managed at
last to sit up and give a yell which woke me up, the
rats burst out from everywhere. I felt as though a flock
of these demons was emerging from my body and
scattering in all directions, screaming with rage. My
hair stood on end, my blood ran cold. My eyes fell on
the figure of my wife outlined against the flames, and
something about the shape of this sleeping form
increased my horror without my being able to understand the reason. When at last I dared to lift my head
and look more closely, I saw one of those ghastly
animals clinging to her forehead, fastening on to her
skin, hanging on to her with all the strength of its
claws. It had planted its fangs into the wretched
woman's nose and its snout was quivering, drenched
in blood. She did not move. She had succumbed to her
exhaustion and I was scarcely strong enough to groan.
Without letting go of its prey, the demon darted a
glance at me with its red eyes. It remained like that
for a long time, threatening me, until my wife eventu-

ally reacted to the pain by bringing both her hands up to her forehead in a reflex of distress.' "

"Stop," I broke in. "My own blood is running cold as well. That's what you wanted, I can see. Well, you've succeeded. But that's enough."

"All I've done is translate Chong's own words for you, sir. He seemed anxious to let us know all the details of his tragic situation. . . . And I don't think you realize yet the exact nature of the peril that was threatening them, at least from his point of view."

"It seems quite clear to me. They were in danger of being eaten alive."

"That goes without saying, sir, just as they were in danger of dying of hunger; for what remained of their provisions excited the vermin's greed to the point of madness. Even though the woman carried their meagre larder on her, the rats had succeeded in breaking into it. Yet, incredible though it may seem, that was not the essential reason for their anguish."

"I don't understand, venerable sir."

"Because, in spite of the facts, you persist in endowing him with your own reasoning, your own instincts, which are those of a normal human being. It was only little by little, through his feverish insistence, that we ourselves finally came to understand the true nature of his horror.

"In his rare moments of lucidity, sir, he was frightened of yielding to temptation!"

"What temptation?"

"He was frightened the agony might become unbearable. He dreaded it might reach such a degree of intensity that they might go out of their minds. He was terrified at the thought that in a moment of weakness he might despatch his assailants with the precious contents of the bottle which had so far been preserved intact in spite of all the hazards."

"The poison," I muttered. "That's true. I never thought of that."

"You would have thought of it if you had been in their predicament. This torture, the mere account of which filled you with horror—do you imagine you would have endured it for over a week? Make a sum total of the suffering represented by fever, sleeplessness, rat-bites, disgust, horror and fear of starvation. Now remember that, as during their meeting with the robbers, they had an easy way of destroying their foes. You'll agree then, I'm sure, that it needed superhuman willpower—outrageous willpower, certainly, but nevertheless heroic—not to make use of this method.

"A handful of rice steeped in the potion would have been enough to poison a dozen rats perhaps. With the bodies cut up and sprinkled anew, they had the means at their disposal of destroying the whole cursed brood in a single night. These animals feed on one another. This would have assured them sleep and rest, and at the same time an almost inexhaustible supply of fresh food, since they knew how to prepare it so as to render the poison harmless."

"I can understand the temptation. And they did not yield to it?"

"Not a drop, sir!"

"I admit, that argues a sort of heroism."

" It was above all when he thought of the possibility of giving in that his mind in an absurd manner identified the rats with the creatures of some unknown hell. This became clear after his many explanations. It's a curious sign of his disconcerting mentality. He regarded these beasts as the instruments of some malevolent jinn who had tried to exploit their instinct and make them succumb to this temptation. By analysing this psychological complex, an expert might, I fancy, discern a hint of method in his madness, in the absence of all logic."

" No psychology, no analysis, venerable sir—you promised me. Only the facts."

" These are the facts, sir," said the old Chinaman, with sudden animation.

" He told us with shame that he had almost admitted defeat. It happened the day he had the vision of the rat devouring his companion's face. At that moment, he told us, he had a moment of despair. He managed to drag himself as far as the corner where their priceless treasure stood. He took out the plug which served as a cork. His suffering was too inhuman. He was about to prepare the liberating bait by sacrificing a little of this fabulous elixir.

" And it was his wife who held him back, sir! She had heard the noise and guessed his intention. She restrained his arm. She placed her sightless face in front of his with such a painful air of reproach that he blushed and felt ashamed of himself . . . I can't control myself when I think of their behaviour. Which of these two was the madder, sir, can you tell me? She,

E

by opposing the only reasonable act he could still accomplish? Or he—he, who felt gratitude and almost religious admiration for this creature? He, of whom it was impossible to tell whether his veneration was due to the tireless devotion of this lunatic or to the gesture which condemned them both to torture? "

My old Chinaman fidgeted on his bench and went on passionately:

" Here are some more facts. She promised him, the better to persuade him, that she would not let herself fall asleep any more. He in his turn promised not to repeat his attempt. And both of them together swore that under no condition would they draw off a single drop of this poison. You may well wonder at the oath by which they both undertook to oppose each other if either of them showed the slightest sign of succumbing.

" They recorked the bottle. And then, sir, at that precise moment, he solemnly assured us, he felt much better! According to him, his recovery had begun at that very second. Naturally he saw in this yet another miracle!

" They both observed the terms of this outrageous pact. And when one of them felt himself weakening, do you know what the other did, sir? Here are still more facts! The more resolute one at the moment, the one on whom the rôle of saviour devolved, would take the bottle and place it silently in his companion's lap—as though it was a sovereign remedy against weakening, one of those relics which sick people are made to touch! And the other would always be grateful for this gesture. He felt the profound significance of it, his courage would return. And, both shedding tears of joy, they would then in turn place their cheek against the icy glass! Two maniacs, sir, two maniacs—there's no other possible description for them, and I'm mad myself to try and think of any other! Two maniacs, that's it— two creatures beyond the confines of our world, whose perverse instincts had been monstrously developed by hardship to such a pitch as to eliminate all sentiment, all desire, all human reaction, to the exclusive benefit of a morbid passion! "

10

"COMPOSE yourself, venerable sir," I said. "Calm down, I beseech you, for your indignation is contagious and I feel that I too am going to lose my self-control. I agree with you, it's a waste of time to try and find a reason for acts of madness. But it's also childish to get irritated because you can't find any; you're the one who's now behaving like a child. Pull yourself together and calmly continue with your account of the facts."

"You're perfectly right, sir. I must ask you to forgive me.

"The rat episode comes to an end with Chong's recovery. He was soon able to get up and share the watch with his wife, and even kill a few of the beasts with his stick. So they had enough to eat and after a few days were sufficiently strong to set off again. And their journey continued. They crossed the highest mountains. They encountered other obstacles, all of much the same sort. I don't think they could be of any great interest to you."

"I've formed a pretty clear picture of that trek, venerable sir, and of the spirit that inspired it. Besides, didn't you warn me that from beginning to end it was a repetition of similar incidents whose philosophical essential can be summed up in a very few words?"

" Yes, sir: hardship, thirst, fatigue and fear—in short, suffering."

" Tests, as Chong put it? "

" Tests. That was the very word he used."

" The sources of hostility being still, I suppose, men, nature and beasts? "

" That's a rather peculiar way of regarding the events, but up to a point it's correct."

" Tests from which they always emerged victorious? "

" Always, sir—by some unheard of chance and as though they were protected by some occult Power."

" That's all I wanted to know, venerable sir. Go on with the rest of the journey."

" It takes us more or less up to the end of the accused's statement of evidence. The rest you know, or can easily imagine. They reached Yi-Ping in the state which I've already described. He resumed his job as assistant executioner under his father. He now proved to be as conscientious and skilful as he had once been careless and clumsy; he was eager, he had vowed, to become a chief executioner. His diligence reaped its reward. His touch became so masterful that shortly afterwards, on his father's death, the high mandarins of the province overlooked his bad behaviour in the past and entrusted him with these functions.

" Then he embarked methodically on his series of crimes, following the plan he had drawn up. The hideous stage-setting was perfectly adapted to it. In the absence of the other officials it was easy for him to keep his assistants at a distance and to pour out the poison. In the shadows he would watch the arrival of the condemned man. He would observe each of his gestures. As soon as the latter had gulped down the glass of alcohol, Chong the executioner would step forward into the full light in his ceremonial garb. His victim's collapse was attributed to emotional shock. He operated in this manner seven times in three years.

"It now remains for me to tell you about the rest of the trial: in fact the trial proper, all that I've dealt with so far being only the preliminary investigation . . . that is, if you're still willing to hear it, of course."

"If I'm still willing, venerable sir? I shan't close an eye, I shan't rest for an instant, until I've heard the charges put forward by the prosecution and the arguments of the defence."

"You shall hear them, sir, but not until tomorrow. I'm sorry to cause you a sleepless night, but I've talked too much this evening and my mind is becoming confused."

I left the city of Yin-Yang in a state of intense overexcitement. As soon as I was outside the ancient town walls I noticed a white form lying by the side of the road, from which there arose a sound of lamentation.

It was my guardian angel. His plumes were damp from the bitter tears he had shed while waiting for me.

"I heard everything," he said. "*Animus meminisse horret*. I forced myself to listen out of love for you—an extremely laudable effort on my part. I am pained and distressed to see you lending an ear to the inanities of that old Chinaman. His two heroes are perverse and

absurd creatures, he admits it himself—criminal
lunatics whose behaviour is an outrage to reason and
moral sense."

" So you, too, are appalled by the behaviour of that
fellow Chong! " I sorrowfully observed. "You too,
like that old Chinaman."

" Well, yes. . . . His raving is the only worthwhile
element in the whole story. But why expatiate on foul,
ignoble acts which everyone condemns? And you, you
whose brain is still malleable, you feast on these
trumpery adventures in which I have searched in vain
for a spark of humanity.

" Ah come back! Come back with me, I beseech you!
I'll lend you new books, and you'll at last be able
to write a real story. I've prepared a long list of
works in which you'll find the nourishment which is
best suited to your youth. You'll choose your characters out of them yourself. You'll write a story glorify-
ing mother love, or paternal love, or filial love, or
conjugal love, or platonic love, or adulterous love, or
incestuous love, or bestial love if you must, but anyway a story containing a little human warmth."

With my mind in a whirl, I drew away from Yin-
Yang and returned with him to the world of moderation.

And next day, shortly before dusk, I made my way
back once more towards the magical city. And my
guardian angel, my faithful guardian angel, kept me
company all the way. And the litany of his advice, his
warnings, his entreaties, accompanied my every step.

And I, in my ingratitude, was insensible to this devotion!

I now feel a flush of shame mounting to my cheeks as I make this confession, but—and I give you my word, this is strictly true—I was beginning to find him slightly importunate. His solicitude appeared hypocritical to me and I found his persistent attempts to impose his exclusive paradise on me tactless. As he begged me for the thousandth time to undergo a cure of disintoxication and to seek asylum in the human species, I had the temerity to reply:

"Now listen, guardian angel. I haven't your experience, but I've travelled quite a bit and met all sorts of people. I don't speak the sacred languages, though I've glanced through a few rose-coloured pages; but when it comes to Chinese customs, my knowledge must be almost equal to your own. . . . After all, what are your qualifications for coming down to Earth and talking to me about humanity?"

"My qualifications? I've a hundred thousand of them."

"A hundred thousand?" I said.

"I've read a hundred thousand books," he declared impressively.

"A hundred thousand books!"

"A hundred thousand books," he repeated, ruffling his feathers. "Ever since I was born, you realize, I've lived in a corner of Paradise. I've furnished it to my taste, and no one comes and disturbs me there. I've blocked up all the entrances. While you were travelling and meeting all sorts of people, I, I'll have you know, forbade myself all distraction. I didn't once put my nose out of doors. I kept myself pure. I fiercely avoided every contact, apart from Letters. I guarded myself jealously against every influence outside my cell that might have hindered my intellectual concentration and interfered with the life—that seething, swarming, sparkling, tumultuous life—which pullulates in my twenty million or so lines that have been written and read.

"My qualifications? My qualifications for talking to you about humanity? Listen to this. I own a vast filing cabinet filled to bursting point with slips of paper : slips of paper arranged in alphabetical order. And on these slips everything, absolutely *everything* of interest to man, is written down, do you hear—all the thoughts, all the feelings, all the wisdom, all the manias, all the intelligence, all the emotions, all the furies, all the uncertainties, all the errors, all the terrors, all the virtues, all the vices, all the *passions* of literature! And you ask me on what authority I speak to you about humanity! "

"Oh, all right," I said impatiently. "Now I'm going to tell you a parable, guardian angel."

"Don't use a word when you don't know what it means," he replied, shrugging his wings.

"An allegory, if you prefer. It's about a friend of mine. His father, who was the watchman of a vast building where some pianos were stored, began bringing him with him to this place at a very tender age. He therefore learned to walk among pianos, which were soon familiar objects to him and which his childish

E*

imagination endowed with a mind of their own. Crawling about on all fours, he discovered the pedals, the legs and, a little later on, the smooth wooden sides which his fingers stroked lovingly.

"His knowledge of pianos gradually became more and more complete. One day, by stretching up on tiptoe, he managed to raise the lid of a keyboard an inch or two. Peering with delight, as though in a dream, at the fantastic tile-pattern of the black and white keys, he had a revelation of beauty. His heart was filled with joy. He often repeated this gesture, without ever daring to lay a finger on the ivories—what delighted him was the majestic calm and silence of these motionless objects.

"His experience soon embraced the piano stools whose slow gyrations were a source of infinite ecstasy to him. He went on growing and, after a few years, had a fresh view of the instruments. He contemplated the top of them, and the great shining surfaces of the grand pianos awakened a poetic instinct in him.

"When his father died, he was given the job of watchman. He went on living among the pianos, enriching his knowledge at every instant by an original angle or unexpected moulding. Frequently, as in the days of his infancy, he would furtively raise a lid to peer at the keyboard with a smile of satisfaction, just as overawed as ever by its cold pure geometry and mysterious silence.

"He lived to a very advanced age, after seeing thousands and thousands of pianos of every size and make pass through the building, for they were frequently changed. No one in the world had an experience of pianos comparable to his.

"Well, believe it or not, guardian angel, but at his death he still did not know how to play a piano. He could not even read a note of music."

"What happened then?" my guardian angel asked.

"That's the end of the story," I said.

"Just another of your stories without head or tail to it. You're trying to lull me to sleep and make me relax my vigilance, for we've now arrived outside the accursed place. Don't go in."

The ramparts of Yin-Yang rose before us. He placed himself in front of me, unfurling his wings. I tried to reason with him.

"Now listen, guardian angel. Let's make a pact. Grant me a few more escapades and one day, when I have more experience, I'll write a story for you, I promise—a story for you alone, one of those stories for which you have established the norm and restricted the scope. It will fit automatically into one of your compartments, under one of your headings—under Thrillers or Psychological Novels, under Novelettes, Tales or plain Accounts, but it won't be betwixt and between. There will be nothing Chinese about the characters. As in real life, they'll act or they'll think, but they won't do both. They will be tender-hearted or harsh, sad or gay, logical or absurd, but I vow they won't be monsters beyond the confines of humanity who weep after just having laughed. . . . Nothing but the probable, nothing but the human, I swear. Heavens, I can see it, I can feel this future work already! You think I'm incapable of writing it? How little you know me! Have confidence in me, guardian angel. I can already reveal the subject of it to you; it will be the story of a tormented heart which seeks its way without finding it and finally despairs. What do you think of that? It will reveal such secrets that anyone will be able to say: 'That's the sensation I had the other day while drinking my coffee.' You'll conclude: 'There's nothing new under the sun,' and, in speaking of me, 'I always said he had it in him.'

"But in the meantime don't be selfish. Let me go in."

"You shan't go in," he said.

I had come in vain to the limit of every possible self-sacrifice. He had not listened to me. His attitude had become threatening. His voice grated like that of an evil angel. I was frightened. . . .

Ah, what more could I say to excuse my conduct? Had I lost all self-possession? Had the fumes emanating from the city of Yin-Yang disturbed my brain? I took a step forward and knocked against him rather violently. He did not budge. I saw his great wings slowly folding back.

I fought. We struggled together. He was the stronger. Inexorably the wings closed round me. In a defensive reaction I clutched hold of them and tried to force them apart. The feathers came away in my hand. I was astonished to see that they were as hard and pointed as daggers. I lost my head. I seized one of them and struck out. A jet of blood spurted. His grip weakened and he slowly collapsed.

I took to my heels without daring to look at him. I

had acted, certainly, in a state of legitimate self-defence
—he might have strangled me on the spot to save my
soul!—but I was rather alarmed all the same. As I
entered the forbidden city, I trembled as I heard a
dying voice bidding me a final farewell.

" *Aeternum vale!* "

Part Three

Part Three

1

" GO on, don't be frightened," I said to the Chinese
doctor. "Don't spare me any fantasy. Today I
can listen to everything. No one, alas, will reproach
me for that any longer."

"I'm delighted to see you so happy, sir."

"I can see you'll never understand me. Why,
I'm overcome with remorse and feel horribly for-
saken!"

"I'm so sorry. I had mistaken your condition for
jubilation. I've never seen you with such a gleam in
your eye. . . . But I'm afraid you may be disappointed
in the end of my story, for it's extremely commonplace.
In fact it's merely the inevitable conclusion to the
adventure. Perhaps, though, there are a few curious
touches to it."

"The touches will console me, I'm sure, venerable
sir. Please go on."

" When Chong had come to the end of his statement,
the President gave him permission to sit down and a
few witnesses were called in. They had no fresh evidence
to add. Nothing of any interest."

"What about the woman, Chong's wife?"

"She was also called in—no further interest there,

sir, either. She was as she had been described in every detail: skinny, a slug-like complexion and a sightless face in which no expression could be seen. To crown these advantages, she was more or less incapable of expressing herself coherently. All that she lacked was to be dumb!

"The Mandarin President spoke to her severely, reproaching her for not having used her influence over Chong to bring him back to the right path. She did not seem to understand and muttered a few unintelligible words. Then he asked her to confirm her husband's main statements; there he managed to drag a little out of her. Chong had not taken his eyes off this creature since she came in. She, in her turn, after twisting her head round in every direction, seeking his gaze, had set her face in his direction. From that moment on no further reply could be dragged out of her In exasperation the Mandarin President dismissed her ignominiously. She disappeared, feeling her way along, and that was the last that was seen of her."

"I see. In any case it would have been mad to expect any further enlightenment from her. What happened next? "

"Let me consult my notes. After that. . . . Here we are: after that the Mandarin President called on the plaintiff to speak."

"The plaintiff? I suppose you mean the Attorney General? "

"Not at all, sir. The Attorney General represents Society. He will be making his appearance later on. I said: the plaintiff—the injured party, if you prefer.

Why are you so surprised? Aren't I making myself clear? What I mean is, the individuals who have suffered damage and are seeking compensation."

"Venerable sir," I quietly said, "this surpasses my wildest hopes. It's difficult to follow you, though. Try and explain yourself more clearly. You never mentioned any plaintiffs before, or their presence at the tribunal."

"I must have overlooked them, and I apologize for that. It's obvious they attended the tribunal."

"But who were they?"

"Well, first of all the families of the seven victims, sir. That was the main group. After that . . ."

"The families of the seven victims! Venerable sir, tell me, tell me at once, in two words, what were their grounds for complaint? You must certainly have jotted down an accurate list of their grievances. I can't be left in ignorance of them a moment longer."

"You seem very overexcited, sir."

"I beseech you, venerable sir. Each aspect of this trial is more precious to me than a leaf of gold."

"Your haste disturbs my plan. Since you're so impatient, however, I'll tell you that the principal complaint of the families was the 'loss of face' suffered by one of their members."

"Loss of face!"

I gave a start, as though a pin had just been planted in my thigh. For a long minute I looked at him with suspicion.

"Yes, sir," he went on in genuine astonishment. "Isn't that the expression which in your language indicates, however imperfectly, a feeling akin to humiliation, to . . ."

" Go on," I said, calming down a little. " I'm a ninny. Do you know, for a moment I thought you were joking. I shan't interrupt you again."

" So much the better, sir. Your agitation, which is incomprehensible to me, disturbs my train of thought. Well, there were the families of the seven victims. . . . All the members were not there, naturally. Each family had appointed a delegate. . . . Then there were the priests of the three cults, and finally a representative of the clan of executioners.

" The families were by far the most considerable group. It alone included several thousand people, who were, moreover, none too respectable, which was only to be expected. In China every profession is pursued within the framework of the family clan. The profession of bandit is no exception, so that the relations of those condemned to death were identified with the miscreants of the district."

" Just a moment," I said, turning this over in my mind. " Since you're such a stickler for order, let's recapitulate. Chong had against him, first and foremost, the whole criminal population—isn't that so? "

" That's so."

" And secondly, Society—that's to say the mass of honest citizens who were to voice the main accusation through the mouth of the Mandarin Attorney General, as you told me? "

" Precisely, sir. And in addition, accessorily, the priests and the executioners."

"Go on, venerable sir. I understand now."

"I'm glad to hear it, sir. Here, then, is the representative of the families. The seven delegates, having similar claims, had agreed to have them put forward by one of their number, the oldest and wisest. His claim contained two points: firstly, he demanded compensation for the damage and grief caused to the families by the death of one of their members. . . ."

"There seems to be a flaw in his wisdom," I observed. "If the words have any meaning, the damage and grief would have been exactly the same without Chong's crime."

"That question gave rise to a lengthy debate. In the end the opinion of the court coincided with yours. In China we all have a strong business sense. We were well aware that the delegate was trying to turn the situation to his advantage, but the judges considered his claim excessive.

"As for the second grievance, it concerned, as I said before, the 'loss of face' inflicted on the members of the clan. This was far more serious. It is quite certain that by preventing the condemned men from carrying out their rôle in the ceremony and showing a manly attitude, the executioner seemed to have a very low opinion of their courage. The tribunal considered the grievance well founded, reserving itself the right to fix an appropriate compensation in due course."

"What sort of compensation were the families demanding, then?"

"A substantial sum of money, and the death sentence for Chong. That accounts for the families, sir."

" I see. And the other injured parties? "

" They were admitted, but only with reluctance, so paltry were their grievances compared to the main accusation.

" The executioners' representative felt that the honour of his profession had been besmirched. He claimed a fine as a matter of principle and, needless to say, the death penalty.

" Then it came to the turn of the three priests. They had to assist the condemned men in their final moments on earth, and Chong's intervention had thwarted them. We listened to them in attentive silence, for, even though we are not religiously inclined, we welcome every doctrine and we appreciate symbols. We enjoy hearing a thesis expounded, and their presence promised us some good entertainment."

" I'm a little Chinese myself on that particular score, venerable sir. What were the theses of the three priests? "

" Quite simple and straightforward. The Buddhist was the first to speak. He explained to us that in depriving the condemned man of his final quarter of an hour of existence, the executioner no doubt prevented him from performing an act of charity, thereby forcing his soul to be reincarnated in the body of an inferior animal.

" The Taoist priest regarded Chong's initiative as the deprivation of a quarter of an hour which was particularly propitious to mystical emotions and profound meditation. Thus the condemned man lost the best chance in his life of entering into communication with the principle which rules the world.

"Some of the Notables took advantage of the situation to ask for a complete explanation on the theory of the transmigration of souls and the precepts of Lao-Tse. We all listened, partly out of curiosity, but above all out of courtesy towards these holy men, who are always somewhat foreign to us and who were in a sense our guests. The crowd was not particularly impressed. We applauded, however, for the sake of politeness, and the bells accompanied this ovation for a decent length of time.

"As for the Confucian sage, he merely said that Chong had violated the Ritual. This was a truly Chinese turn of phrase and cheers broke out spontaneously throughout the courtroom.

"After they had explained their doctrines one after the other, they all three came to the conclusion that Chong had failed in every one of them. They therefore agreed to demand a communal compensation—the death sentence.

"These, sir, were the claims of the plaintiffs. The Mandarin Attorney General then took them into consideration, while putting forward his own at the same time. I made a note only of his peroration. It's remarkably clear in its concision and, moreover, sums up his entire speech. Here it is:

"'. . . In conclusion, Notables, Chong's guilt is manifest.

"'From the strictly juridical point of view Chong had on seven occasions violated the Chinese law which forbids killing. Each of his acts, according to our Code, has a precise qualification. This is not a case of simple homicide. The weapon he used is enough to dispel that illusion. . . . It's the coward's weapon—poison. It's a clear case of intentional murder, a premeditated crime and punishable by death.

"'Chong, moreover, has introduced an essentially disturbing element into the traditional order established by our ancestors. This fault, serious enough for an ordinary individual, assumes a sacriligious character when committed by a mandarin, no matter how small, whose duty is precisely to respect the ritual. For this misdemeanour Chong the executioner is equally liable to the death penalty.

"'Let us now sum up, Notables, the particular circumstances which attended these acts. My task, though painful, is easy, for Chong has accused himself. I shall merely confine myself to drawing your attention to his cynical statements.

"'He has told you the occasion on which the instinct to kill was born in his brain; but he was incapable of giving a single motive which might explain, if not excuse, this desire. No passion, no fury, blinded him. He bore no particular grudge against the men condemned to death. He therefore acted out of sheer perversity.

"'He conceived his crimes several years before committing them. Think of that, Notables. For more than forty moons he lived with this thought in mind, and during all that time he never had a twinge of shame, not even a reaction of pity for the victims he had chosen and condemned to die with such appalling composure.

"'To hypocrisy he added evil-mindedness, pretending to repent and submit to the will of his father, whereas he was only guided by the desire to kill.

"'Finally, Notables—you will have noticed this, as I have—since appearing before us, Chong has shown no sign of remorse. We were all expecting, you were hoping as I was, for a word of regret, a gesture, a mere impulse of humanity, which the vilest murderers have at the recollection of the wretches whose existence they have implacably cut short. We were disappointed. Chong the executioner appears, on the contrary, to pride himself on his conduct.

"It is therefore my duty, Notables, to demand the death sentence for Chong.'"

"I suppose," I said, "that the drums and bells marked the solemnity of this moment as usual?"

"Scarcely, sir. There was no sensation. This conclusion was only to be expected, and our curiosity was distracted by the approach of the next development—the advocate's plea."

"I'm in the same frame of mind, venerable sir, I must admit. I carry my love of paradox to such lengths that I am dying to hear the arguments put forward by the advocate in defence of such an untenable cause."

2

"THIS advocate was a knowledgeable sage himself, sir, reputed for his wisdom, his wiliness and also for his talent for discovering arguments which had occurred to no one else. He did not disappoint us. I also think that he'll satisfy your desire, which I think I discern, to witness a brilliant mind and more than average learning put to the service of the most execrable iniquity.

"Here is the advocate. He collects his thoughts. He greets the mandarins and the Notables ceremoniously. He begins as follows:

"'Notables, I wish first of all to take up a purely juridical stand. I am going to permit myself in all humility to contradict certain conclusions of the illustrious Mandarin Attorney General. He has presented Chong's case as a clear one. And so it is in fact, but I shall show you that its clarity is not what he fancied it to be.

"'For this, it is necessary for me to read you a few documents, which no one has so far mentioned in this case in spite of their importance. You know them well. I merely wish to recall them to your memory and ask you to weigh up each phrase in them when you come to decide on my client's fate.'

"At this stage, sir, he paused for a moment, while

the court sat silent, intrigued by this opening and impressed by his composure. Eventually he drew several scrolls of paper from his wide sleeves, unrolled one of them and started reading:

"'Judgement of the High Court of Yi-Ping, dated the . . . Whereas . . .'—I'll leave out the unimportant details—'The Court, with the concurrence of the Notables, declares the accused Lee guilty of murder, denies him the benefit of extenuating circumstances and *sentences him to death*. . . .

"'This,' the advocate remarked, 'is the sentence passed by the tribunal as the conclusion to the case of the accused man Lee. Lee, I would remind you, Notables, was the first condemned man to be executed by Chong: the object of his first crime according to the prosecution's contention . . . *The sentence passed by this court*, I repeat, Mandarin President. This official document is signed by Your Honour. It is likewise initialled by you, Notables, and witnessed by the illustrious Mandarin Attorney General.'

"At that moment, sir, I noticed, a barely perceptible murmur betrayed the pleasure which began to grip the public, and their hope. The Chinese man in the street, who is sharp-witted, realized that this reading of the document and this insistence on dotting the 'i's and crossing the 't's augured some special entertainment. He discerned some surprising development, without knowing exactly what the advocate was leading up to. Mystery added to his pleasure."

"I think I can discern it fairly clearly myself," I said.

" I congratulate you. . . . But don't spoil my pleasure, for I'm re-living this scene with passion.

" The advocate methodically put his scroll away, unrolled another and started reading again:

" 'Judgement of the High Court of Yi-Ping, dated the . . . Whereas . . . The Court, with the concurrence of the Notables, declared the accused Sao guilty of murder, denies him the benefit of extenuating circumstances and *sentences him to death*. . . .'

" 'Sentences him to death, Notables,' he repeated. 'This term has a remarkably precise meaning which cannot be disputed and to which I would ask Your Graces to give the closest attention. Sao, I must remind you by the way, is the second victim which the prosecution attributes to my client, the executioner Chong.'"

" I had guessed as much, venerable sir," I said.

" We all had some notion of it, sir. But we were grateful to the advocate for taking this line, for letting his intentions sink in gradually, of their own accord, by infusing them with a grisly atmosphere of uncertainty. The murmur of the crowd, which now accompanied each of his gestures, became slightly more pronounced when he was seen to unroll yet another scroll and prepare to read it out loud."

" I wager it was to do with the third man condemned to death."

" Yes, sir."

" And the sentence was identical? "

" The sentence was identical, word for word."

" In that case, venerable sir, it's superfluous to read it out again. I, too, am breathless with curiosity, and we're wasting time. Let's proceed to the seventh judgement."

"Sir, I am pained to witness such impatience. In China we like to savour our pleasures slowly."

"I can understand that, but you yourself are destroying the effect of surprise. Go on, I beseech you."

"So be it, since you disdain refinements. I shall go straight on to the seventh sentence.

"'The Court, with the concurrence of the Notables, declares the accused Yuan guilty of murder, denies him the benefit of extenuating circumstances and *sentences him to death.*'

"The advocate paused once more. He waited, in an attitude of the most profound meditation, for these seven successive readings to take their effect. Then he went on:

"'This is recorded by brush, in black on white, with legally prescribed ink and in the form laid down by the Ritual. This is approved and signed by every one of you. May I now be allowed in all humility to put a question to the members of this tribunal? I ask you, Notables, I ask you, learned Mandarin President, I ask you, illustrious Mandarin Attorney General, if any of you contests the authenticity or validity of these documents?'

"'No,' replied the mandarins. 'No,' replied the Notables. 'No,' replied the Mandarin Attorney General. 'These documents, we guarantee, are perfectly authentic and valid.'

"'May I further ask if there is anyone among the same members of this august Court, if there is anyone who feels today in his Just man's mind that these sentences are illegal or contrary to equity? '

" ' No,' replied all the officials with one voice, and with still greater insistence. " No, certainly not. These are good, just and equitable sentences.'

" ' I note your sage reply,' the wily advocate went on in a rather more solemn tone, ' and I thank you for it.

" ' Now this is the honourable Mandarin Attorney General's point which I take leave to contradict. He has said: Chong bears full responsibility for his crimes. The urge to kill was in him. He premeditated his offences on his own. . . . Is it not, on the contrary, clear to you in the first place that this desire, this intention to kill, should be ascribed to the signatories of these sentences and, secondly, that this desire and intention conform to the law both in spirit and to the letter—this law which, according to the prosecution, has been violated? '

" Scarcely had he finished speaking, sir, when the drums and bells broke out at full pitch, indicating the emotion and voluptuous intellectual excitement of the assembly."

" You were quite right, venerable sir," I observed. " If the conclusion of your story is simple, its finer shades, as you led me to expect, are full of curiosity. This advocate fascinates me. Don't stop. What did he say next? "

" Nothing, sir, for quite a long time; for the drums went on rolling, the bells ringing, and a brisk agitation reigned in the courtroom. The magistrates whispered in one another's ears. The President exchanged irritable signs with the Attorney General. The advocate stood motionless, his head bowed, his arms folded across his chest, his hands concealed in the sleeves of his robe, in an attitude of extreme deference.

"It was the Mandarin Attorney General who first spoke as soon as order was re-established. He was visibly overwrought, which diminished his prestige in the eyes of the crowd. He did not seem to be in possession of his usual self-control. He declared:

"'The eminent advocate, Notables, is trying to sow confusion in your mind in an underhand manner. Do not allow yourselves to be swayed by his dialectic. The case is clear, I repeat, and all his efforts are merely designed to obscure it. The law of the province of Li-Kang is specific and allows for no exceptions. No one has the right to make an attempt on the life of his fellow-man. Chong has killed. Chong has admitted acting with premeditation. Chong has committed seven murders. The blood of his seven victims cries out for revenge.'

"The advocate then turned round slightly and, with his usual composure, addressed himself to him directly:

"'I see I have not succeeded in convincing my honourable contradictor. Am I to understand that, in his eyes, the seven condemned men are *victims*? '

"'Precisely,' the Mandarin Attorney General stoutly declared. 'Victims.'

"At this point, sir, the Mandarin President opened his mouth as though he was about to speak. He cast a furious glance at the Mandarin Attorney General, but the latter in his excitement failed to notice.

" ' I crave his indulgence for my insistence,' the advocate went on, without allowing his rival to say a word, ' but I must ask him to be even more specific. Does he consider that the individuals Lee, Sao, Yuan, etc., were killed contrary to our sacred rites? Does he assert that the act which cut short their life is a culpable, inhuman act and must be punished by law— that is, literally murder? '

" ' Without a shadow of doubt,' the Mandarin Attorney General heatedly exclaimed, adding, ' Life is a gift from heaven . . .'

" ' I take note of that, Mandarin President,' the advocate broke in, raising his head again. ' I see that the illustrious Mandarin Attorney General is fiercely opposed to the death sentence. The sentences passed by this tribunal, which I had the honour to read out to you, he considers illegal, inhuman and criminal.'

" At this the Mandarin Attorney General flushed, sir, and tears came into his eyes as he protested violently, even forgetting the rules of politeness.

" ' Not at all! ' he shouted, clutching the rail in front of him with his clenched fists. ' The advocate, Mandarin President, is trying to lend a perfidious sense to my words. I never meant that. It is beyond all doubt, it is only too obvious, that Society as represented by this tribunal has the right and duty to condemn guilty men to death. But this is the case of an individual . . . an *individual*, Notables, that's my point and I would ask you to bear it in mind. I maintain that no individual has the right to act as an instrument of Justice.'

"'Not even a mandarin in the service of Justice?'
the advocate enquired, raising his voice slightly.

"'Certainly not!' the Mandarin Attorney General
stormed. 'He least of all. A mandarin is paid to
administer the law, not violate it.'

"'Not even the executioner?'"

"Look out, it's a trap!" I in my turn shouted, caught
up in the turmoil of this debate.

"Be quiet, sir. . . .'

"'Not even the execut . . . !' the Mandarin
Attorney General burst out.

"Then he stopped in mid sentence, I noticed. He
went scarlet in the face, a deeper red than his ceremonial robe. The fantastic convulsions of the
embroidered dragon on his breast betrayed the palpitations of his heart. His hands trembled. Beads of sweat
broke out on his forehead, turning the colours of his
make-up into a greyish paste. His false beard seemed
to bristle under the effect of his indignation. His skull-
cap was askew. His pigtail hung down, lamentable and
inert, like a grotesque and obscene symbol revealing,
for all to see, that he was about to lose face shamefully.

"The two rivals stood facing each other amid the
tumult of the drums and cymbals, accompanied by the
shrieks and stamping of the crowd. The spectacle, sir,
was rare to behold. The Mandarin Attorney General,
it must be admitted, was not in a strong position. The
craftiness of the defence had put him in a state of rage
which was unusual for a Chinese dignitary and which
made him ridiculous in the eyes of the people. He had
fallen like a child into the trap which you discerned.

F

The advocate, it is true, had shown diabolical cunning and conducted the debate with the manifest intention of putting him out of countenance. He had prepared this new effect with extraordinary talent, speaking first of all in a very quiet, almost humble tone, then gradually raising his voice and thundering out his last reply: 'Not even the executioner!' with a flutter of sleeves which caused an intoxicating draught. He had humiliated his contradictor unquestionably, and the Chinese showed their enthusiasm with loud cheers. Chong's cause had gained ground in the mind of the crowd, but the mandarin magistrates and the Notables looked uneasy and irritated.

"This is how the advocate continued his attack, sir, as soon as the storm had abated a little:

"'Not even, great mandarin, when the executioner acts on an order signed by you, like an obedient little mandarin? Not even when he carries out *to the letter* the prescriptions of these other documents which I shall now read out to you and which are likewise signed by you? Here, for example: the condemned man Lee, the condemned man Sao—there are seven of them, Notables, the seven alleged victims of my client—the condemned man Yuan will be handed over to the executioner. He will take charge of him and *proceed with his execution.*

"'And proceed with his execution—that, too, is written down in black on white, Mandarin President, The words of the Chinese language have one meaning only. Far be it from me to try and obscure this debate, as my honourable contradictor has accused me of doing.

On the contrary, I wish to restore to it the schematic
simplicity which his wisdom refuses to perceive, because
it wanders off on points of detail. I shall lay the question bare before you and you will see it revealed in all
its stark purity.

"'To sum up the juridical aspect of this case: con-
cerning these so-called victims, there was a sentence
passed by you, an unassailable and utterly equitable
sentence, condemning them to death. There was subsequently an order, likewise given by you to the executioner Chong, an order which his duty *forbade* him to
shirk—the order to execute those condemned to death.
Chong, as a mandarin respectful of the law, took charge
of these condemned men and took their life. Chong
executed them. He was an obedient, irresponsible and
innocent instrument. He acted legally and cannot incur
any punishment.'

"That, sir, was the argument put forward by the
advocate from the strictly juridical point of view."

3

"THERE'S a really able advocate," I remarked.

"Yes indeed. He was extremely clever—a little too clever even, and in the end he failed to win his case."

"You don't seem to appreciate his arguments?"

"They are what are known, I believe, in your language as sophisms and which you the other day, to my mortification, referred to as *chinoiseries*. I admit that many Chinese are partial to them—the applause of the assembly showed this only too clearly. But that sort of reasoning, which is attractive enough at first glance, always has a point of extreme weakness which neither art nor eloquence can conceal indefinitely. The whole edifice collapses as soon as one puts one's finger on this point.

"The President adjourned the hearing—a wise measure which allowed the Mandarin Attorney General to recover his composure and think things out. On resuming, he had no difficulty in refuting the advocate's thesis, as you shall now see."

"I beseech you, venerable sir, first of all satisfy my curiosity. What was the accused doing all this time? You haven't mentioned him again. What was his attitude during this verbal tussle?'

"Incomprehensible, sir. He didn't intervene at any

stage. His face expressed complete indifference. He was apparently the only one to take no interest in this battle of wits. His gaze was once more fixed on the ceiling, so much so that the Mandarin President, who was slightly vexed by the advocate's manoeuvres, called him to order and dryly enjoined him to show a little more respect. All to no purpose—he maintained this detachment right up to the very end.

"After the adjournment, then, the Mandarin President, who had turned the matter over in his mind and re-adjusted his dress, had no difficulty in destroying the specious argument. He begged leave to speak and said:

"'Notables, the plea of the eminent advocate is brilliant, but it is only a plea. He is confusing—intentionally, I'm sure, for he is too skilled to do so by mistake—two acts which have nothing to do with each other.

"'Acting on the orders of the tribunal, and according to the ritual laid down by the law, the executioner fulfils a legal function, whereas the individual Chong, by anticipating the executioner's gesture contrary to this ritual, commits a murder. That is the whole crux of the matter. Chong cannot be regarded as the instrument of Justice since he did not make use of the proper instrument: the sword. Your sentences did not prescribe poisoning and therefore cannot excuse him. This is quite clear to all of you, and it is useless for me to offer further proof. I shall merely quote an example of a striking analogy: a soldier who brings down his foe in war time acts legitimately, whereas he is a murderer if he kills the same individual before the declaration of hostilities.'

"This was the voice of reason. The assembly showed that they were satisfied by giving a long-drawn murmur. The advocate's intervention had entertained them for a moment, but the wise Chinese people, though they enjoy being carried away for a short while by the attraction of intellectual fantasy, know how to pull themselves together in time and come down to earth again very quickly. The advocate realized he would never be able to topple this massive battlement of common sense. From then on he appeared spiritless. He had emitted all his sparks in one fell swoop, like those fireworks whose fuses go off simultaneously. The Chinese accord them a passing acknowledgement, but they show their real esteem for a better maintained household.

"But, realizing now that he had won the day, sir, the Mandarin Attorney General in his turn gave evidence of diabolical ingenuity. Listen to this final, terrible shaft he hurls at his opponent:

"'Not only, Notables, did Chong not obey your orders, but he surreptitiously *prevented* the execution of your sentences. Through his fault the condemned men Lee, Sao, Yuan, etc., *did not undergo* the punishment which you saw proper to inflict on them. They therefore did not atone for their crime, and Justice was thwarted yet again. I would ask the tribunal to bear in mind this additional crime which I had omitted and which the plea of the eminent advocate suggested to me.'"

"Enough," I begged. "I beseech you, venerable sir. No Westerner can hold out for long against such an orgy of ingenuity, not even me. I ask for mercy. My head's in a whirl."

"It's all over, sir. But, for the Attorney General to have his revenge, it was necessary for the advocate to lose face in his turn. This is what happened, and the public applauded his defeat as warmly as it had celebrated his victory.

"Honour was saved. The game had ended in a draw. All the mandarins heaved a sigh of relief; then, out of politeness, they gave their attention to the two opponents' respective points of view. They analysed them, they dissected them, and there was a general discussion during which all the articles of our Code were brought up. I shall spare you all this, for it can't interest anyone but a specialist. In conclusion, as was only to be expected, the Court decided in favour of the Mandarin Attorney General, but mitigated the humiliation of the advocate by rendering homage to his ability and talent.

"Foiled on the juridical plane, he then pleaded insanity, as I told you. It was the only possible defence. If Chong's attitude had not made such an unfavourable impression on the Notables, he might have had a chance of winning them over, for it was a fine speech he gave."

"The advocate also believed his client to be insane," I muttered.

"At all events he pretended to think so, and his tone was sincere. Listen to this, for instance:

"'Are you fully aware, Notables, of the acts which have brought my client here? The murder of some

wretches already condemned to death and with no more
than a quarter of an hour to live. No one can seriously
maintain that this is the behaviour of an individual of
sound mind. The Mandarin Attorney General has
declared that Chong could not possibly have had any
grudge against his victims. I, for my part, would add
that he had no *interest* in doing away with them. He
had nothing to gain from their death. The only conclusion is that he is insane. There's not a shadow of
motive for his crimes."

" Still this question of motive," I said.

" Still the same question, sir. The advocate did his
duty and tried to exploit this mystery to the full. He
showed that Chong's insanity dated back several years;
that it was provoked by the emotion of his attempted
suicide, by the death of the dog and by an inexplicable
dream. According to him, Chong had been living ever
since in a state of hallucination. As proof, he put forward that senseless journey of his and his morbid
attachment to that bottle. To cut a long story short,
he did his utmost to turn the most unfavourable of his
client's statements to his advantage.

" But, as the Mandarin Attorney General pointed
out to him once more, absence of motive did not necessarily argue insanity. On the contrary, taken in con-
junction with such logical reasoning as Chong's, with
a willpower as strong as his, and a persistently evil
intent which overcame all obstacles, it could only
perhaps be attributed to one state of mind—perversity."

4

"IT was this word, *perversity*, sir, that put the finishing touch to the case. It was to this that all the hypotheses that could be erected in this affair led back."

"I shall now come to the conclusion—which you have already guessed, I am sure."

"You can be quite sure," I muttered resentfully. "Don't worry, Satan, I recognized you long ago. I've let you have your say, but you haven't deceived me. I smelt the fire and brimstone as soon as you appeared. Finish your job. Tell me the conclusion. I'm sure it will fulfill all my hopes and reinforce my optimism as to human destiny."

"Your language, sir, is incomprehensible, but I shall do as you wish.

"Chong the executioner was condemned to death. No other sentence could have been given. The entire population of Li-Kang cried out for his head, even the lowest strata of the population who would not forgive him for having chosen poor destitute wretches as his victims. The corps of Notables was unanimous. Thus the case came to an end.

"But I should like to come back just once more, sir, to the mysterious question of motive. It prevents me from sleeping at night, I must confess, and I cannot resign myself to classifying it among the insoluble problems."

My old Chinaman had assumed an attitude of profound meditation. His eyes reflected the dark infinity of abysmal spiritual depths. I admired him in spite of myself. He made me think invincibly of Rodin's *Penseur*. He appeared to me as the personification of human genius in its painful and eternal struggle towards greater lucidity, towards a more and more intimate communion with the glorious secrets of the Universe.

"Everything has been said, sir, on the subject of these extraordinary crimes. Everything was said, I know, at the hearing and at the sages' discussions. The infamy of that fellow Chong surpasses the limits of one's imagination, I grant you. But none the less, the fact remains, he was a *man*. I examined him several times, as a doctor, and with passionate interest, as you may well imagine. He was normal from the psychological point of view. He showed no pathological strain, and several of my psychiatric colleagues assured me of the integrity of his mental faculties. He was, as I said before, a human being, constituted and organized to all outward appearances like every other Chinese person —like you and me, sir."

"Like you and me, venerable sir," I pondered.

"And as long as I live I shall maintain that a being of that sort must always obey a motive, no matter how fantastic it may be. There is a cause for every one of his acts. That is the essential difference between our voluntary movements and the reflexes of wild beasts. Don't you agree? "

"Between us and wild beasts . . . I agree with you entirely, venerable sir."

"Well, sir, in spite of all the efforts of the tribunal, the mystery remained unsolved.

"Each time he was referred to this subject, Chong harked back again and again to his hallucination. He digressed on his so-called mission. But on the *why* of his frenzy, he still shed no light at all. Towards the end of the final hearing the Mandarin President advised him several times, in his own interests, to make a complete confession on this point, as he had on all the others. The Notables made the same request. The advocate, when he saw the case was lost, sided with them, for he knew that his client's refusal would entail a more severe sentence than the simple death penalty. We Chinese do not like the irrational, and the less we understand something the more severely do we punish it.

"All their efforts were wasted, sir. Every now and then, however, Chong seemed to make a genuine effort to explain himself, as though he was trying to interpret a difficult truth, but it never came to anything."

My old Chinaman's expression underwent a further change. His tone became almost solemn as he tried to extract the philosophical essence of his story. No doubt this was a further ruse of his. He belonged to a race which beats drums and rings bells to mark the emotional stages of existence. But the artifice of his attitude aped the signs of genuine emotion so closely as to be taken for them.

"He took his secret with him to the tomb, sir. No one will ever decipher it now. Maybe he was sincere, after all, when he appeared to struggle as he did with an inexplicable mystery? Maybe he was not sufficiently educated, not sufficiently knowledgeable, to grasp the real reasons for his behaviour? Maybe, too his silence was the will of heaven? Maybe those reasons were of a too atrocious nature to be uttered out loud? Maybe the universal order forbade the scandal of a revelation which might have inspired weak minds with unwholesome ideas?"

"Maybe . . . maybe he didn't want to blow his own trumpet?" I said.

The old man looked at me with an expression of alarm.

"Sir, you sometimes make remarks which baffle me, but I can't help wondering whether you're not a bit of a cynic."

"Don't bother about me, venerable sir. I don't exist . . . I thank you for your story. It's simple and strange, as you promised. But one of your last statements surprises me, I must admit. You said something about a punishment more severe than the simple death penalty. Does this mean you've got another subject of wonder hidden up your sleeve?"

He slowly stretched out his hand and seized his chopsticks which he had laid down beside him. He began manipulating them with a dexterity that could only be described as prodigious. I was reminded of a gigantic crustacean armed with delicate pincers.

"That's correct, sir," he said. "But I don't know if I ought . . ."

"Finish your job," I cried. "Let's have it all. I want to drain the cup to the dregs! "

"If you insist. . . . This is it:

"Just think, sir. Everyone was too indignant to be satisfied with a simple decapitation. Public opinion cried out for an exemplary punishment. Furthermore, the plaintiffs had not been able to obtain the financial compensation to which they were entitled. Chong was a poor man. They had to be given compensation. In matters of repression, as in all other matters, it's the finer shades that distinguish civilized nations. The high mandarins therefore decided to inflict one of our old-world punishments on Chong.

"It is, I believe, a punishment peculiar to China—a protracted one, to which we only have recourse in the most serious cases. Our ancestors, who invented it, succeeded in endowing it with a character at once shameful and painful, thereby adding humiliation to mental agony.

"Chong expiated his crimes, sir. I give you my word, the punishment was in proportion to the offence. I don't see any point in describing this scene to you, but if you like . . ."

"Satan! " I yelled. "I recognized you, I tell you. You would be quite capable of treating me to all the refinements of Chinese torture, just to crown your impertinent story! I don't want to hear about the tortures at any price. Stop waving your chopsticks about like pincers. Take your claws out of my heart. I've no more curiosity. I'm satisfied with your accursed tale. . . . I'm certain, after having heard it, that the punishment was in proportion to the perversity! "

" Have no doubt on that score, sir. I can vouch for it better than anyone else, since I witnessed it."

" You witnessed it! "

" From start to finish, as a medical expert. The tribunal had renewed its confidence in me, in fact, after sentencing me to a small fine. I did my best to acquit myself worthily and was careful to avoid all negligence. Although it was extremely long, I assure you I did not let my attention stray for a single second.

" You may be sure, too, that this time no one disturbed the order of the ceremony. As you can well imagine, the precedent of Chong was a salutary warning and the new executioner was closely supervised. Extraordinary precautions had been taken to avoid any untimely intervention. Chong remained fully conscious right up to the moment ordained by the Ritual."

The old Chinaman pulled himself together and, as I mopped my brow, finally added:

" Moreover, in my opinion, sir, these precautions were superfluous. Creatures like that fellow Chong are exceptional and few and far between. They are not common phenomena, which is lucky for us. According to Chinese statistics, they only appear at the rate of one every two or three thousand years. And they commit crimes that are so monstrous, so contrary to every human instinct, that they never encourage disciples."